A footstep on the stairs. Another.

She raised the gun. Two-hand stance. One foot pushed slightly back. Well balanced. Just as her father had taught her.

Another step.

Gaia aimed the gun at the level of the doorknob. Waist-level for Natasha. That was another of her father's instructions. Always keep a gun aimed at the center of the body. Don't go for anything fancy like a head shot; just make sure you connect with the target. If Natasha rushed her, Gaia could drop the gun and fight. If Natasha was carrying a weapon, Gaia could shoot.

She was ready.

Don't miss any books in this thrilling series:

FEARLESS™

Available from SIMON PULSE

FEARLESS™

BLIND

FRANCINE PASCAL

SIMON PULSE
New York   London   Toronto   Sydney   Singapore

First Simon Pulse edition May 2002

Text copyright © 2002 by Francine Pascal

Cover copyright © 2002 by 17th Street Productions, an Alloy, Inc. company.

SIMON PULSE
An imprint of Simon & Schuster Children's Publishing Division
1230 Avenue of the Americas, New York, NY 10020

 Produced by 17th Street Productions,
an Alloy, Inc. company
151 West 26th Street
New York, NY 10001

Printed in the United States of America
10 9 8 7 6 5 4 3 2 1

Library of Congress Control Number: 2001097510
ISBN: 0-7434-4399-3

To the best fans:
Emily, Kathryn, Lucy, Maddy, Meg

Instead of
life with
Gaia, it **broken**
had turned
out to be **glass**
the start of
life After
Gaia. Ed A.G.

GAIA UNFOLDED THE NOTE AND

squinted at the words for the twen-
tieth time. She had to take a few
steps down the sidewalk and hold
the note up under a streetlamp
before she could see well enough to
read.

Spider Gaia

TOM MOORE, APT. 1801, ABERDEEN BLDG.

Pretty sketchy note. Whoever had slipped the piece of paper under Natasha's front door was a long way from Tolstoy.

Since finding the paper that night when she'd come home, Gaia had folded and unfolded the sheet so many times that the little piece of paper was already starting to wear thin along the creases. Another couple of hours and she'd have nothing left but some ragged confetti.

Gaia raised the note and squinted at the sloping handwriting in the poor light, trying to see if there was some secret she might decipher from the six short words. Had her father written the note? Maybe. She couldn't tell. The letters were scribbled, which could mean whoever had written the note had been in a hurry. That could mean someone was after the note writer, and that could mean it had been written by her father. Sure. And it could have been written by Santa Claus. Maybe with a little help from his pal, the Easter bunny.

Gaia scowled at the letters until the message started to blur. Was this an invitation? Was her father asking her to meet him at this location? It was just as likely—probably *more* likely—that her uncle had written the note and that the thing was nothing but an invitation to get herself neatly dissected under a microscope. That was, assuming her uncle really was the killer Loki. Gaia didn't know that. Not for sure. She took one last look at the note, then jammed the paper into the pocket of her jeans. She wasn't sure of a damn thing these days.

If mysterious people were going to drive her crazy with cryptic notes, Gaia wished they could at least leave a decent address. It had taken two hours online before Gaia was able to locate the Aberdeen Building. By the time she'd climbed up out of the subway on the west side of Central Park and hunted through the maze of apartment buildings and brownstones, it had been close to five in the morning. Even with an address, it had taken another twenty minutes to identify the Aberdeen as a skinny, twenty-story affair that looked out of place among a crowd of newer and much shorter duplexes.

Gaia stopped on the corner and watched the building as cabs rolled slowly by on the narrow street. Despite its height, the Aberdeen had a weary, worn-down look about it. The building was faced with some kind of gray stone, which had grown smeared and dark from years of air pollution. There were carvings at the corners. Big gray faces. They might have been faces of presidents, or famous explorers, or rich old farts who had put up the cash for the building. Whoever they were supposed to be, they all had a serious case of `acid rain acne` and were too eroded for Gaia to make out much more than hollow eyes and grim expressions.

She counted narrow balconies along the flat front of the building until she found the eighteenth floor. Most of the rooms were dark, but some were light. Gaia wondered who would be awake at this crazy pre-dawn hour. Maybe her father. Or a killer. Or both.

Either way, Gaia hoped for some answers.

She hustled through the traffic and up onto the sidewalk in front of the Aberdeen. When she reached for the worn brass handle on the front door, it unexpectedly flew open, and a man in a dark red uniform stepped out. "Yes?" he said through a muffled yawn. Clearly, Gaia was interrupting his nap. "Can I help you?"

Gaia studied the man for a second. There was some kind of unwritten rule: The shoddier the building, the more elaborate the doorman. This guy looked like he was ready to lead French forces at the

Ardennes. Or maybe the British in the Boer War. He looked almost old enough to have been at both battles. His red wool uniform was several sizes too big for his buzzard shoulders, and the long, sweeping coat brushed the tops of his boots. Gold braid spilled off the brim of a ridiculous felt hat. There was even something that looked like medals jangling against the man's pocket. Gaia wondered what kind of medals a doorman might get. The Silver Star in taxi hailing? The Purple Heart for bad Christmas tips?

The doorman stepped completely out of the old apartment building and let the door swing closed behind him. "You want something here?" he asked, folding his thin, uniformed arms across his thin, uniformed chest.

Gaia shrugged. "Just visiting."

"And who is it you were visiting at this hour?"

"My father. He has to catch an early flight and I'm here to see him off."

Sounds plausible.

"Your father, is it? And what would his name be?" The doorman had an accent that sounded like Dublin by way of a decade in Brooklyn.

Gaia started to say something, stopped, and tried to think. What name would her father have used?

"What's wrong there, miss? Don't you know your own father's name?"

"Moore. His name's Tom Moore."

The doorman's colorless lips puckered. "I've not heard of him."

"What about Oliver?"

"Mr. Oliver?"

"No, Oliver Moore."

The man shook his head, sending the gold braid on his cap into a dance. "Never heard that name, either." He squinted at Gaia with pale gray eyes. "You sure you've come to the right building, miss?"

Gaia gritted her teeth and stared through the glass door behind the man. She could see a long, marble-floored hallway leading back to a pair of elevators and the old metal button between them that would take her up to her father. "This is the right building," she said. "My father lives here, and I want to see him." She started to move around the doorman, but the old man stepped back against the door and shook his head again.

"You can't come in. Not unless someone inside says it's okay."

"My father—"

"I don't know your father," said the doorman. "You give me a name I know and I'll ring a bell, see if someone wants you on the inside; otherwise you need to get out of my door."

The muscles in Gaia's jaw tightened into a painful

knot. The pleasant idea of kicking the man's bony ass down the street came and lingered for a few moments in her mind. Reluctantly she shoved it away. She had no doubt that she could take this guy out with both hands behind her back and blindfolded. But the doorman was just an old guy doing his job. A sour old guy, yeah, but that didn't mean he deserved to get his ugly wrinkled face turned inside out.

Gaia turned away from the door without another word and marched back along the sidewalk. She heard the old man give a grunt behind her. He sounded awfully satisfied with himself. Maybe he would get another medal. The Medal of Doorman Honor for keeping ignorant kids out of the building.

As soon as she was around the corner, Gaia stopped. She tipped back her head and looked up the long side of the building. She could see the first few floors well enough, but the top was nearly lost in dingy gray fog and darkness. Eighteen floors was. . . what? Two hundred feet? Something like that.

It was one of those moments when fear would have been handy. It would have been nice to know if the decision she was about to make was very brave or just really, really stupid. But there was nothing. Not even one of those gut-grabbing jolts she'd been having ever since her uncle had tried to cure her of fearlessness.

Gaia crouched down, her fingers touching the cold

surface of the sidewalk. Then she jumped up, reaching for the gray face at the corner of the building. Her left hand closed on the damp, worn stone and she pulled herself up. It wasn't until she was looking into the hollow eyes of the oversized face that she realized she was holding on to the carved nose.

Gaia laughed, which cost her a foot of climbing. She worked her fingers into a gap between two of the building's sandstone blocks and scrambled against the stone with the toes of her sneakers. A few seconds later she was standing on the face and reaching up for the lowest of the balconies. From the second floor to the fourth she clung to a rusty drainpipe. It made Gaia think of how she used to climb up the drainpipe into her bedroom at George and Ella's brownstone by Washington Square Park. That was, what? Three months ago? Less? It seemed like forever.

The drainpipe headed off at the wrong angle above the fourth floor, but Gaia found a crack barely big enough for a finger jam and a narrow band of marble that ran along the building between floors. The marble strip made for a treacherous ledge, barely more than a fingernail wide, but Gaia was able to jump from there and catch the bottom of the fifth-floor balcony. She pulled herself up and rested for a moment. Through the window she could hear someone's radio alarm blaring the weather report. They were expecting rain.

Perfect timing. Coming inside from the rain, plopping down on a couch, and listening to a little morning show seemed like a rather attractive idea at the moment. Gaia grinned as she thought of what the people inside would think. Surprise. Your fearless neighborhood Spider Gaia is here.

A series of raised stones made travel easy from five up to the tenth floor. Another narrow marble band got her to eleven, where it was so dark, Gaia had to do more feeling for holds than looking. The tips of her fingers began to get sore from rubbing against the rough stone.

She remembered a climbing trip with her father when she was ten. Clean mountain winds somewhere up in Vermont. Warm pink granite gleaming under spring sunshine. She glanced down. Not exactly Vermont. The dark street was more than a hundred feet below her. There was one insomniac out walking his dog, but he didn't look up. People in New York never looked up. They were too afraid of being mistaken for tourists.

On her way from eleven to fourteen—Gaia figured that an old building like this wouldn't call any floor thirteen—she reached a new set of faces. The faces looked especially weird up here, with all the light coming from the street lamps. The eyes were deep and dark, the mouths open. The face right in front of her looked mad and kind of hungry. *So this is what it feels like to step on someone.* Gaia shook her head and mentally corrected herself—it was just something else to climb on. She jumped up and grabbed for the granite face.

The nose snapped off in her hand.

For a long second Gaia could only stare at the broken bit of granite in her hand. *Grab the reins, Gaia, it's an inanimate object.* She scrambled wildly, fingers scraping against the rough sandstone, her feet seeking anything that might stop her fall. She tumbled down, falling back from the building as she plummeted past the twelfth balcony. Head down, she saw the sidewalk coming up toward her face. Fast.

Gaia felt something like a dull icicle stab into her heart. *Oh, sure, now Oliver's magical mystery brew decides to kick in.* Her stomach made a mad run for her throat.

A wild kick and she managed to jam a foot through the railing on the eleventh-floor balcony. The sudden twist and jerk on her leg was so hard that she was sure she had broken it. A moment later she forgot all about the pain in her leg as her body smashed against the side of the building with such force that all the air burst from her lungs.

Oh, yeah, she thought. *That was graceful.*

She dangled there by one aching leg for long seconds. Her heart was beating hard enough that she swore she could hear it. Her breath was coming in needle-sharp gasps.

Why was it I wanted to feel fear? The feeling she got from the serum never showed up when she needed it. It only put in an appearance right at the moment when Gaia needed to be thinking clearly.

It took at least a minute for Gaia to recover, `bend like a jackknife,` and make her way back up to the balcony. Her leg hurt. Her hip hurt. Her arms and back and head hurt. The fake fear feeling slipped away slowly. Ready, no doubt, to make a return visit when it was needed least. Gaia made a mental note: In retrospect, the decision to climb the building seemed more on the stupid side of the line. She'd have to remember that for the future. Then she reached her increasingly sore fingers up and started climbing again.

On this second pass she avoided the cracked face on her way to fourteen. More worn stones gave her an easy ride to fifteen. Another pipe made the trip to sixteen easy.

Halfway to seventeen the rain came.

Not bothering to drizzle, the weather went straight from dry to downpour. Gaia glanced up and saw the pale reflection of the city's lights against the bottom of the clouds. In the distance the sky grew bright with a tangle of lightning.

"Perfect," Gaia said aloud. "Absolutely perfect."

The wet stone was suddenly five hundred percent more slippery under her grip. There was no pipe making an easy road up to seventeen. No fat and simple cracks in the stones. Gaia hung on like a lizard clinging to a wall. Her fingers and arms trembled. She climbed as much with the muscles in her stomach as the muscles in her legs.

The balcony on seventeen was enticing. Gaia even thought of going inside and making her way to the eighteenth floor with genuine stairs, like a human being, but there were sounds from the other side of the glass door. Sounds that showed there were two people inside. At least two. Gaia shook her head and looked out at the flickering lightning. At least somebody was having fun on this ugly night.

She left the moaning and panting behind and headed up the final stretch to eighteen. Fortunately the building was more worn here, the blocks of stone curved at the edges and the gaps wide. Gaia had no problem finding enough handholds and footholds to get herself up the last ten feet to the next balcony. Once on eighteen she crouched on the balcony for a few minutes to catch her breath. She had started to open the door before she noticed that someone had put numbers on the door handles. This was 1803. She glanced to the side. The next balcony was close, not more than six feet away. A short jump.

Brave or stupid? She looked down. This decision was simple. If she made it, it was brave. If she splattered on the sidewalk, it was stupid.

Gaia climbed on the railing and made the jump. It was an easy jump if you could ignore the wet, slippery railing and the two hundred feet of nothing that waited for anyone who might screw up.

Apartment 1801 was dark. Gaia pressed her ear against the cold glass of the balcony door. Nothing. Only the soft hiss of rain against the building and the distant sound of traffic down below. She grabbed the door handle and pulled. It was unlocked.

A nearby flash of lightning momentarily lit the room, and Gaia felt, more than heard, a rumble of thunder that came right on top of the light. In that split second she saw that the apartment was small, just a modified studio, with a half wall that separated the kitchen from the rest of the living area. She caught the impression of a table and a couch, a few odds and ends of furniture. And she got the definite idea that she wasn't the first visitor to the apartment. Disappointment washed over her. She might find some answers in this place, but if her father ever *had* been here, he was certainly long gone. She took one slow step into the darkness, felt along the wall for a switch, and flipped it on.

The apartment looked like a shipwreck. The cushions had been torn from the couch and the cloth slashed open to reveal ragged cores of dingy white foam. Books and papers were strewn everywhere. An armchair was overturned, a coffee table broken.

Pictures had been pulled from the wall. Refrigerator and cabinet doors hung open, and all their contents, from bottles of soda to bags of flour, had been spilled onto the center of the kitchen floor like the ingredients for some huge and nasty recipe.

Gaia waded into the room, her sneakers crunching on broken glass. The place reeked. There was a sour, spoiled-meat smell—from the mess in the kitchen, she hoped—and above that the sharp, acrid odor of smoke. She navigated through the piles of broken furniture and heaps of ripped books and traced the fumes back to the wisps of smoke rising from inside a small metal trash can. It was clear that whoever had destroyed the apartment had done it very recently. She reached into the can, pulled out a stack of blackened, smoldering paper, and flipped it back and forth through the air. A few sparks flew off from the sides before the smoke stopped rising.

"All right," she said. "Let's see what was worth making such a stink."

The first few sheets where hopeless. The paper flaked away into dust as soon as she touched it. At the back of the pack a single page had survived. The paper was charred black at the top, and there were a few holes on the page, but the rest was only a toasty brown. In these lighter areas Gaia could make out. . . something. She held the scorched page close to her face and frowned. The first part was a mess. Some kind of code. The rest didn't even look like writing. There were no letters that she recognized. Instead, what was left of the page was completely covered in three repeating symbols. A green delta. A red cross. A blue circle. A brown square. The symbols sprawled right up to the right edge of the paper. In the burned areas she could make out glossy spots where more symbols had been.

Gaia stared intently. Some new kind of code? She was good with codes, always had been, but this was unusual. Four symbols, over and over, and what looked like random combinations. How could she translate this?

She lowered the page and gave the metal trash can a sharp kick. The can turned over, spilling gray ash onto the floor. Smoke started to rise from the bland, tan carpeting, but Gaia stomped it out before it could become a real fire. She stirred the black mess with the toe of her shoe and saw something else that had escaped total consumption by the flames. She reached in and pulled out a Polaroid photo. Like the paper, most of the photograph was blackened. The plastic covering over the picture had bubbled and turned brown. In the shadows that remained, Gaia could barely make out the silhouettes of three people, but she couldn't see any of their faces clearly enough to say who they were. Gaia and her parents? Tom and some friends? There was nothing but dark, somewhat eerie shadows.

"Wonderful." Gaia sighed and looked around the room. A half-burned page full of nonsense and a half-burned photo of three ghosts. Not exactly the kind of answers she had been hoping for.

Gaia, this is your old friend Disappointment.

Disappointment, you certainly remember Gaia. You've met her so many times.

It took half an hour for Gaia to sift through the mess on the floor and check around the room for something the messy visitors might have missed. If there were secrets hiding in this place, they were evidently staying secret. Finally Gaia found a plastic bag that was half full of crushed soda cans.

My father, she thought. *Sure, he's a spy, a liar, and probably a killer, but he recycles.* She dumped the cans on the floor, put the burned photo and page of symbols into the bag, and stuffed the little package into her coat.

She gave a moment's thought to climbing back down the way she had come up, then shook her head. There was plain stupid and *really* stupid, then there was gargantuan stupid. Gaia gave a last look at the wrecked apartment, flipped off the lights, and went out into the hall to ring for an elevator. She stopped at the door on the way out, turned, and gave the doorman a quick, fierce hug.

16

"The party was great," she said. "Thanks for the invite."

Gaia didn't bother to look back and see the expression on the old man's face. She just hunched her shoulders against the rain and kept walking.

Idiot in Russian

THUNDERSTORMS AND CRUTCHES DID not mix. The rubber tips on the ends of the steel-and-wood contraptions weren't exactly nonslip under the best of conditions. In the rain they were about as useful as racing slicks on a snail.

"Are you sure you want to walk around in this weather? he asked.

Tatiana looked at him and flashed a bright smile. "You said we could look around the park today. I've walked around Moscow in worse weather.

"Besides," she began, but Ed could see her struggle as she tried to translate her thoughts into English. In only a few weeks her speech had already become more fluid, more casual, but she still had trouble digging out the perfect word. "I have you to take care of me."

"Oh, yeah. Sir Limp-a-Lot." Ed knew he wasn't the

world's most likely protector, even if it did feel good to have a pretty girl say that she was counting on him. And Tatiana was extremely pretty. Ed held up one crutch and waved it through the rain. "Bad guys beware."

Tatiana put her hand on Ed's shoulder and let it rest there for the space of several heartbeats. "I can't think of anyone else I would rather have looking out for me."

Ed stared at her hand. Buzzers went off in his head. `Warning. Warning. Physical contact.` What was Tatiana doing? This wasn't supposed to be an official date. Friends only. Strictly casual.

"Uh, Tatiana. . ."

She took her hand away and gave him a soft smile. "Are you ready?"

Ed looked into her wide eyes. There was an expression on her face that he couldn't quite read. "That depends. Ready for what?"

"For a walk around the park, of course."

"One cold, dark walk coming up." Ed could still feel the spot where she had rested her hand on his arm. It probably didn't mean anything. Tatiana was from Russia. People in Russia probably did a lot more touching. It was just a friendly thing.

He looked up at the drizzle falling down around the nearest streetlight. "We're going to get wet."

"It's only water," said Tatiana. "I don't think I will drip."

"You won't what?"

"Drip. Like an ice-cream cone when it gets hot."

"Melt." Ed couldn't help but grin. "You won't melt. You're way too. . ." He was going to finish with "sweet," but then he realized how `pathetic and corn-ball` that sounded. Like something from a really awful black-and-white movie on the Family Channel. Like something from a guy who was desperate to be in love. Only this wasn't the right girl.

He cleared an irritating lump from his throat. "You sure you won't be cold?"

"Cold? Here?" It was Tatiana's turn to smile. "It's practically summer here compared to back home." She held out a blue umbrella and pressed a button on the shaft, and the canopy opened into a wide dome. "Besides, I have this to keep the rain away."

"Okay," said Ed. "We'll just make a quick lap now and then come back when the weather's better, okay? It'll be more entertaining then."

She nodded, her blue eyes bright. "Yes, that sounds perfect."

Ed started up the sidewalk with Tatiana close at his side. The wet sidewalk limited how fast he could move, but Tatiana didn't seem to mind. She paced along beside him, holding the blue umbrella above them both.

Some NYU students shouldered past Ed and ran on into the rain. Most of them weren't wearing coats.

It wasn't that cold. Or that wet. Ed knew that New York was capable of infinitely worse weather. So why did today seem like such an *über*-suck?

They crossed the street and turned toward the park. How many times had Ed walked this way with Gaia? Fifty? A hundred? However many it was, it wasn't nearly enough. He liked Tatiana, he really did, but no one could take the place of Gaia. Even if lately she had been using his heart for a hacky sack.

Halfway down the block they slowed to get around a crowd waiting near the door of a small restaurant. Tatiana peered through the tall windows as they passed. "Do they have very good food there? Is that why everyone is waiting?"

"That's Jimmy's Burrito. The food is. . ." Ed shrugged. "It's cheap. I guess it's good. Not exactly your five-star place. It's one of Gaia's. . . I mean. . ."

"Gaia likes to eat there?"

Ed nodded. "Yeah, sometimes."

Tatiana stepped away from him long enough to stare through the window. She wrinkled her upturned nose. "You are sure this food is good?"

Her expression was so cute, it immediately restored Ed's smile. "It's at least as good as borscht," he said.

She pouted. "Borscht is. . . how you say. . . sucks?"

More cuteness. "Sucks? I thought all Russians loved the stuff."

Tatiana nodded with mock seriousness. "Oh, yes. And. . ." She glanced around for a moment and dropped her voice to a whisper. "We are all spies."

Ed laughed again. "Then maybe I need someone to protect *me* from *you.*"

Tatiana was quiet for a moment, then she leaned in and planted a quick kiss on Ed's cheek. "Maybe you do," she said. She raised the umbrella high and started forward. "Come on. Show me the park."

Tatiana walked on, but Ed didn't move. He stood there leaning on his crutches as though the tips had somehow sunk into the concrete. *She's Russian. She's only being friendly. Like hell.*

Tatiana stopped and looked back at him. "Are you coming?"

Ed nodded. *Why couldn't I have met her six months ago?* he wondered. He caught up to her and slipped under the cover of the blue umbrella.

Could it really be only days since he'd had sex with Gaia? It seemed like something from another lifetime. Something from a movie that he had seen once but could barely remember. Gaia had been there, right next to him, warm and soft. He remembered waking up and finding her in the bed. He remembered the smile on her face and the way the sun had slanted through the window and burned against her hair. That morning had seemed like the start of a whole new life. And it had been. It just wasn't the life Ed had expected. Instead of life with Gaia, it had turned out to be the start of l i f e A f t e r G a i a . Ed A . G .

Ever since that morning, she had treated him like he was suffering from some kind of plague. Every time he tried to find out what was going on, she only pushed him farther away. Ed felt more isolated from Gaia than he had on the first day he had seen her.

Lightning flashed as they approached the street corner. The sudden flare caught Tatiana in profile, illuminating her pale hair and lending a strange fire to her blue eyes. For a moment she seemed taller. Different.

"What's wrong?"

Ed shook his head. "For a second there you looked just like—"

"Like who?" asked Tatiana. Her eyes were narrowed to slits framed by dark lashes.

Ed swallowed. *Like Gaia.* "Different is all."

Tatiana continued to look at him for a moment. A smile came slowly to her face, but it was tentative. "Thank you," she said, but her eyes were still narrow. Ed thought she probably had a very good idea what he had been about to say.

"The park's right over there," Ed said, hoping to distract her. He pointed toward the dark brick walls and the looming trees with the rubber tip of his left crutch. "We can cruise around the block, and I'll—"

"No," said Tatiana. She looked at the park and

shook her head. "You were right. It is cold. We can go to the park another day."

"So. Do you want to. . . go home?" Ed asked with a shrug.

She nodded. "I think I should."

For two blocks they walked along in painful silence with only the sound of rain thumping against the umbrella. A steady stream of cars swam past in the street, sending up twin plumes of water. The people they passed seemed as gray as the evening.

Ed abruptly stopped. "Tatiana, I'm sorry."

She studied him with her head tilted slightly toward her right shoulder. "You still love Gaia, don't you?"

Ed winced. "It's that obvious, huh?"

"If there is a word that means more obvious than obvious, then that is the word to use," said Tatiana. She took one hand away from her umbrella and put it on her hip. "But Gaia has been so rude to you."

"I know."

"She treats you badly. You deserve better."

Ed sighed. "I guess maybe you get treated the way you let yourself get treated. With Gaia. . ." He hesitated and stared at the ground. "I wanted her for so long."

Tatiana let the umbrella fall to the side. Cold drizzle fell down on them both. "I don't know why Gaia acts the way she does. She's hurt you so much already.

I think that if you keep this up, she's only going to hurt you again."

"Probably." Ed raised his head and looked at her from between strands of damp hair. "How do you say 'idiot' in Russian?"

Tatiana tapped a long, slender finger against her chin. "Idiot. Idiot. Ah! I believe the word is 'Ed Fargo'." She took his arm, squeezed it, and smiled.

Memo

From: G
To: L

Subject has left the target area.
Reconnaissance indicates that the planted
material has been removed. Request instruction
for next phase. Additional assistance may be
required, as subject's habits continue to be
irregular.

Memo

From: L
To: G

That material should ensure the subject
follows another blind alley. Proceed with
delivery of additional material and evaluate
subject's response. Continue observations.
Resources will be made available. It won't be
long now.

But in the
absence of
their leader,
the M&M twins

dangerous

dangerous

seemed to be
verging on
mental anarchy.

A STORM HAD PASSED THROUGH

during the night. Lines of
driftwood and brown seaweed **Spearfish**
along the beach marked how
far the gale-blown waves had
reached, but now, under the morning sun, the sea was
almost glassy.

Tom Moore sat on a clean patch of sand and
stretched out his legs until the heels of his brown
Paloma loafers were lightly touched by the gentle
surf. The sun warmed his face, and his surroundings
were reflected in the lenses of his aviator sunglasses.
It was a small bay, no more than half a mile across,
and the beach was small, too, but it was a beautiful
space. Tall palm trees curved out into the bright air
above the sand. Dark patches on the impossibly
turquoise water marked knots of coral reef just
below the surface. Off to one side a stack of sun-
bleached, faintly pink shells showed where both
locals and tourists had fished conchs from the water.
It was exactly the sort of place where people came to
relax and enjoy themselves.

Tom wasn't relaxed.

He reached down, picked up a handful of sand,
and let it trickle away through his fingers. In books
and films it seemed that secret agents were always
ending up in places like this. How many movies had
there been where James Bond spent time on the

beach with some bikini-wearing babe? All those chase scenes on motorboats and fights on yachts. Agents in films seemed to get in a large share of yacht time.

Tom's life had certainly not worked out that way. It seemed to him that for every hour he had spent in sunshine, there had been at least two spent in shadows. Letter drops in the basement of some Chicago high-rise. Meetings in a Moscow alley. Midnight assignations in Abu Dabi. Being an agent, a successful agent, was about keeping yourself inconspicuous. It was easier to hide where it was dark.

It had only gotten worse over the last few years. The years without Katia. Since her death there had been more dark meetings, more travel, and more lurking in shadows. Tom turned over his sandy hand and looked at the back. Thirty minutes on the beach, and he could already tell that the sun was starting to redden his skin.

That's what happened when you dragged a mushroom out into the sunlight.

He wondered where Gaia was at that moment. It was a thought that often crossed his mind. Probably the thought he had more frequently than any other. Being away from his daughter was. . . It was almost like losing his wife, only not as sudden. Losing Gaia was an ache that went on and on.

That was why he was here, so far from everything

and everyone he considered important. If Loki's plan could be discovered, if his agents could be neutralized, if Tom could ever be sure that Gaia was completely safe, then he could go home again. He could get back to Gaia and try to salvage something that looked like a normal life.

He had been down here for days, trying to find the tag end of Loki's organization. So far his progress had been slow. Loki had taken steps to cover his tracks. All Tom had been able to turn up were the names of a few agents that might—*might*—be working for Loki. He was going to need more information to find the next link in the chain.

Tom took another glance down the deserted beach. What would it be like to come to this place on an actual vacation? To get some of those drinks with funny, tropical names and little umbrellas, toss some towels down on the sand, and soak up so much sun, it drove out all the years of hiding in shadows? He might even get Gaia to shed her grungy sweatshirts. They could be a real family, he, his daughter, and—

His thoughts were interrupted by a splash out in the bay. A small, dark shape broke the smooth surface of the water. A moment later the shape was revealed to be the head of a man with a mask on his face and a snorkel alongside his ear.

Tom waited until the man was stepping free of the waves, then stood and brushed the sand from his neatly creased khaki pants. "Good morning," he called.

The man pushed the mask back from his face and gave a quick nod. "Yah," he said. "Good morning."

There was a certain stiltedness in the man's voice, a trace of accent that put a hard *g* sound in the middle of *morning*. *German,* Tom guessed. *Or maybe Austrian.* Not that it mattered. He put his hands in the pockets of his pants and strolled closer.

Meanwhile, the man had stopped at the edge of the waves and dropped onto the damp sand. There was a black nylon web belt around his waist. Several fish hung from the belt: some snapper, a couple of grouper. Red fish blood ran over his leg and stained the tan beach. The fisherman took off the belt and laid it to his side, then took a blue anodized speargun from its holster and put it down beside the fish.

"That's quite a catch," Tom said.

"Yah," said the man without looking up. He pulled his knees toward his chest and started to remove the fins from his feet.

"I guess there must be a lot of fish out there." Tom took another step, and his shadow fell across the man.

The spearfisher finished taking off his fins and looked up at Tom. The man had short black hair coated with something that was clearly impervious to water. Even after going out under the waves, the man's scalp was still covered in a forest of sharp little spikes. The guy was tall, with broad shoulders and well-cut muscles that spoke of a lot of time working out. He had a deep tan broken only by a small, pale scar at the corner of his mouth. It made the man look as though someone had once caught *him* on a hook and line.

"Yah, yah, yah. There are a lot of fish," he said with obvious irritation. "It is the ocean. That's where they put the fish."

Tom smiled. "Hey, I guess that's right." He looked out at the water for a moment and nodded. "Sure is a pretty spot."

The man with the spiky hair gave a disinterested grunt. He stood up, the belt of bloody fish in one hand and his speargun in the other. "Did you want something?"

"It's just. . ." Tom gave a shrug. "I was wondering if I could see your spray gun."

"It's called a speargun."

"Speargun, right. I've never seen one like that, and I thought maybe I could take a quick look."

The question caused the man to roll his pale eyes, but he pushed the blue speargun toward Tom. "Here, be careful not to shoot yourself."

Tom turned the device over in his hands. "Gee, this is fascinating." He took the safety band from the gun and pulled it aside. Then he touched a finger to the tip of the spear. "Sharp."

"Be careful," said the man. "That gun is ready to fire."

"Really?" Tom pointed the gun toward the ground and pulled the trigger.

There was a sharp grunt of escaping gas, and a plume of vapor rose up in the warm air. The man with the spiky hair continued to stare at Tom for several long seconds, then slowly looked down. Ten inches of shiny metal spear were still visible. The rest was buried in the man's foot. "Uhhh. . . Uhhh. . ." The man looked up, looked down again, looked up, and a shiver ran through his body. "You. . . shot. . . me. . . ."

"Wow," Tom said calmly. "Sorry about that." He reversed his hold on the speargun, got a good grip, and smashed the weapon into the man's face.

The man with the spiky hair screamed. He staggered back, one foot still pinned by the spear, and windmilled his arms through the air. The belt of dead fish went flying as the man fell to the sand. "What are you doing?" he cried.

Casually Tom reached down, grabbed the exposed length of the spear, and gave a quick tug. The man screamed again as the spear came free. Tom took the spear, loaded it back into the gun, and pressed back the firing mechanism. "These gas-powered guns are amazing," he said. He lifted the speargun one-handed and let his aim move over the man's body. "I wonder if this thing would go all the way through an arm. Or what it would do to a knee."

"You're crazy!" The man did a little crab crawl backward.

"Naw." Tom shook his head. He crouched down beside the bleeding man. "I'm only curious. I need a little information." He tapped the sharp point of the spear against the man's leg, and the man did another crab step away.

"What is it you want?" His accent was stronger now. *What* was transformed into *vot*.

"I'm looking for a woman."

The man gave a weak smile. "You want a woman? I know many women on this island."

"I bet you do. The woman I'm looking for is named Noel."

"Noel? That name is not—"

The point of the spear was suddenly hard against the man's forehead. "You know," Tom said softly. "I don't know if this thing would penetrate a head as hard as yours, but I'm willing to try."

"Wait! Wait!" The man ducked away from the spear, covering his head with his hands. "I think I know this woman Noel."

"Think?"

"I know her." The man nodded quickly. "Yah, I know her."

"Then you can tell me where to find her."

"Red Bay. There is a bar called The Rip."

"Rip."

The man nodded. "The Rip. Yah."

"And I'll find Noel there?"

"Every day she is there."

"I've got another name for you. The name is Loki. Noel works for him."

"Loki?" The man had a puzzled look on his face. "I don't know."

The man might be lying, but Tom didn't think so. This guy was just a thug. Hired beef. If Tom was going to get to Loki's Caribbean operations, he was going to have to find an operative farther up the chain of command. Someone like this woman, Noel.

Tom gave the man a bright smile. "Well, okay, then." He straightened, took the speargun, and flung it as far as he could into the warm, turquoise waters of the bay. "You be careful if you go back in the water. An injury like that one on your foot, you might attract sharks."

It was still a beautiful morning. A nice breeze kicked up from the Atlantic side of the island, and the palm trees began to sway.

One step closer to taking Loki down. One step closer to giving Gaia a normal life. Tom squeezed his eyes shut as he walked up into the shade of the trees. He tried not to hear the man crying on the beach behind him.

A is for apple. *B* is for. . .
Who gives a damn what *B* is for?

All I know is, school is for
sleeping. Think of it as an
experiment in alternate learning
techniques. You've seen those
programs that are supposed to
teach you things in your sleep,
right? You know: Slap this CD in
the machine, pop under the cov-
ers, and eight hours later you'll
stop smoking, or lose fifty
pounds, or learn demotic Greek.
They say it on TV, so it must be
true.

Funny, of the lectures that
buzzed past while I was off in
dreamland, I've remembered,
well. . . absolutely nothing.
Maybe I've soaked in some odd
chunks of learnage without realizing it, but I doubt it. I have
concluded that if you fall asleep
with a pen in your hand, you're
probably going to wake up with
ink in places you don't want it.
Results of my experiment: Sleeping
in school is not the best thing

you can do to further your academic career.

So generally, if you're looking for a recommendation, I would vote against it. But sometimes— when, for example, you've been out all night jumping tall buildings in a single bound or maybe just climbing them with all the skill of a monkey on crack—you need to catch a short nap. Short like all of calculus. Maybe half of history.

It probably wouldn't have been necessary if I could have relaxed and caught a couple of hours of sleep at home. Only there were a few problems on that front. First, I was missing the home part. There was this house on the Upper East Side and I did have a room there, but it was Natasha's house, and the room was clearly a loaner. Natasha's was just another place where my father had ditched me. The latest convenient kennel for an unwanted daughter.

Hey, Gaia, here's your new pal

Natasha and her irritatingly
smart and pretty daughter,
Tatiana. See you—I'm out of here.
Maybe I didn't get it word for
word, but I think that's a fairly
accurate transcription of what my
father said before he left.

A week ago I didn't even know
the people that I'm now living
with. And that points directly
to sleep problem number two: I
don't trust Natasha and
Tatiana. Okay, Tatiana did help
me kick a little ass when I
made a slight mistake. And my
dad must have trusted Natasha;
otherwise he wouldn't have left
me with her.

But my dad also left me with
his friend George, and George's
wife, Ella, turned out to be the
leading candidate for the new
Wicked Bitch of the West. In the
end Ella died for me. Weird, but
worth a lot of points on the
trustworthy scale. That didn't
make living with her any fun.
Any way you want to measure it,
my father's record in selecting

foster care does not look so
good.

My advice: When you get to the
point where you're more relaxed
in calculus class than you are in
your own bed, it's time to consider moving.

ECONOMICS WAS ALMOST OVER BEFORE

Gaia remembered to look around for
Heather. She made a sleepy survey of the
class, but at the moment the Village
School seemed to be blissfully Heather-
free. Gaia felt a twinge of guilt. Not a big twinge. A
day without Heather Gannis was not exactly Gaia's
idea of a day without sunshine. But lately, for whatever weird reason, Heather seemed interested in
turning over a new leaf—which apparently meant
befriending Gaia.

Now Gaia needed to talk to Heather about her
new boyfriend, Josh Kendall. She needed to convince Heather that Josh was dangerous. Not dangerous in that leather-jacket-wearing, high cheekbones,
darkly brooding, bad-boy way. *Dangerous* dangerous. Josh might be gorgeous, but he was also
a killer.

Gaia had thought that Josh was dead until she saw
him with Heather. She still didn't understand how
Josh *wasn't* dead. Maybe he was some kind of clone. It
wouldn't be the first time he had been. She already
knew about at least two Josh clones. Would number
three be that surprising? Or maybe his whole death
had been faked. Either way, Josh was walking around
the city, breathing air when he had no right to be and
making out with Heather.

Gaia had already made one attempt at warning

Heather away from him. That discussion had not gone exactly the way Gaia had hoped. In fact, it had been handled with such typical Gaia diplomatic skill that, instead of Gaia's convincing Heather to stay away from Josh, Heather had ended up believing that Gaia wanted Josh for herself. It was tempting to leave Heather alone. But Gaia couldn't do that again. The last time she'd tried to warn Heather of imminent trouble, Heather had blown her off. Gaia had backed down, and Heather had ended up getting stabbed. Heather could be a pain in the ass, but that didn't mean she deserved to die.

The bell rang. Gaia stretched and rubbed away fresh eye boogers as she headed into chemistry lab. Heather and Gaia were in the same lab group for chemistry, which should have generated both a chance to chat and some high-quality awkward moments, but there was still no sign of Heather among the test tubes and stained Formica tables of the lab. However, she was most definitely missed by the others in attendance.

Gaia was barely through the door of the lab before Melanie Young came running up to her. "Where's Heather?"

"I thought it was your day to watch her." Gaia dropped her books on the lab table and stifled a yawn.

The answer failed to thrill Melanie. She looked over Gaia's shoulder and did a scan of the room, as if she were expecting to find Heather hiding in a corner.

"We've got a big experiment today, and Heather... You know, she always..."

Carries you losers, thought Gaia.

"Organizes things," said Melanie.

Gaia saw Megan Stein, the other member of Heather's little chemistry coven, approaching with a similar look of panic on her face. Megan and Melanie were both part of Heather's sprawling entourage, the adoring Friends of Heather. Gaia didn't know much about Melanie, but Megan was in a number of advanced classes and had a good grade point average. It was assumed she had something that looked like a brain. But in the absence of their leader, the M&M twins seemed to be verging on mental anarchy.

In most cases Gaia would have been overjoyed to watch them twitch. But ever since that time Heather had forced them to go undercover to help Gaia out of a rough patch, she'd felt somewhat indebted towards them. And now, since they were all in the same lab group, their bad grade was her bad grade. "It's all right," said Gaia. "I'll do the stupid experiment."

The relief on their faces was in the range of gratitude usually reserved for doctors who had just performed some lifesaving surgery. Gaia ignored the pathetic display. She slipped on a pair of always flattering lab goggles and picked up the guide sheet from the chem teacher's desk. As the other groups formed and started to work through the steps of the experiment, Gaia grabbed an armful of glassware and got to work.

The experiment was actually interesting for once. Starting with a small sample of DNA, a series of chemicals was added that would cause the DNA to break into fragments and duplicate. Eventually what had started as an invisible droplet would grow into a large, stringy mass. Like most high school experiments, it wasn't exactly Nobel Prize material, but to generate so much DNA that you could really see it with your own eyes sounded sort of cool to Gaia.

Melanie and Megan scurried to bring chemicals and watched as Gaia titrated the mix by slowly dripping in reagents from a tube, but soon enough they wrinkled their noses and leaned away from the fumes. Heather might not be present in body, but she was certainly present in spirit.

There were several steps to the experiment, and Gaia lost herself in the complexities. For a few minutes she actually managed to forget about warning Heather, stopping Josh, missing Ed, and wondering if her father or her uncle was really to blame for all the misery in her life. Step by step she walked through the instructions, focusing on nothing but the task at hand. Melanie and Megan brought over the materials as Gaia asked for them. Otherwise the two chatted on about something else through the whole class. Gaia didn't pay enough attention to even guess what they were talking about.

Ten minutes from the end of class, the beaker full of DNA was boiling along like a miniature pot of tea over the blue flame of a Bunsen burner. Gaia leaned over to read the instructions for the final steps of the experiment.

Some background information on the sheet caught her eye. DNA was made up of four amino acids. Only four. There was enough information in a DNA strand to hold the pattern for a virus, a person, a tree, or a monkey. And for all the incredible variety of life, it was all based on only those four chemicals.

Gaia stared at the words. She let go of the glass rod she had been using to stir the DNA mix and picked up the lab sheet. Adenine. Guanine. Thymine. Cytosine. She mouthed the names silently to herself. There was something nagging at the edge of her brain. Something that wouldn't quite come clear.

It wasn't like this was totally new information to Gaia. She knew the basics of how DNA was formed. Science hadn't been the number-one subject in her father's program of accelerated learning for freaky smart and fearless children, but there had been enough. So what was it about this lab sheet that was making telephones ring in her skull?

"Gaia!" shouted Melanie. "Is it supposed to look like that?"

A pungent odor told Gaia what was wrong even before she looked down. The fluid had boiled dry. All that was left of the DNA the experiment was supposed to generate was a brown lump baked hard on the bottom of the Pyrex beaker.

"It's ruined!" said Megan.

Melanie leaned in closer. Her brown eyes looked frog large through the lab goggles. "We're going to get a bad grade on the lab." She turned her plastic-lens glare on Gaia. "I thought you said you knew how to do this."

Gaia started to make some comment, but before she could get the proper words to her mouth, she grabbed for the lab sheet and looked at it again. Adenine. Cytosine. Guanine. Thymine. ACGT. Gaia turned off the gas burner and flipped off her goggles.

M&M were saying something. Gaia ignored them. She closed her eyes and visualized the long, twisting strand of DNA. In her mind the whole thing was shaped like some kind of exotic key. If only she could remember where she left the lock.

"MS. GANNIS?"

Greek Tragedy

Heather looked up and blinked in an effort to clear her eyes. She had slept through the first class of the day, gotten dressed during the second, and munched on aspirin during the third. By fourth period she had judged herself ready to face the world. If only the world wouldn't insist on being so bright and noisy. "Um. . . what?"

A hand came down quickly and snatched the sunglasses away from her face. "We are not allowed to wear sunglasses in class," said Mr. Hirschberg. "You should know that."

Heather held in a groan. The light in the room was so, so bright. Like being on the inside of the sun. And every little photon of that light seemed to be traveling straight into her skull, where it was instantly transformed into agony.

"Sorry," she said through gritted teeth.

The teacher stared at her for a moment longer. Then he gave a slight shake of his head and carried the sunglasses up to the desk at the front of the room. "You'll get these back at the end of the day."

Heather rested her head in her hands and let her dark hair fall forward to curtain her eyes. She had thought her headache was easing up. But it had turned out that the headache had only been hiding, waiting to ambush her the moment she sat down at her desk. She wished she kept a small drill in her purse. Just to drill one small hole, right in the middle of her forehead. Something to let out the pressure. Maybe a pencil through the eye would do.

At the front of the class Mr. Hirschberg began to

explain some tedious detail of that perennial favorite, *Oedipus at Thebes*. Heather moaned to herself as the chalk screeched across the board. Greek tragedy was definitely the right class for her. It seemed like her whole life was becoming some kind of Greek tragedy.

Heather rubbed at her aching temples and tried to think over the previous night. Everything seemed a little weird and shadowy. She remembered being with Josh and walking through the park. There had been some drinking, a few pink poodles. But they were just cute little drinks. Nothing she'd ever imagined could be the cause this level of damage. Nothing that could explain the chain saws and sledgehammers at work behind her eyes.

Suddenly, an ugly image flashed before her eyes. She remembered that she and Josh were getting ready to have sex. Had he suggested they do it in the park? Had she gone along with it? She could hardly imagine ever agreeing to anything so trashy, yet she did have a faint recollection of them fooling around on a park bench.

She must have been wasted. The mere thought of it disgusted her—letting herself get drunk enough to act like a complete dirtbag in public. Had they done more than get ready? Had there been sex? Remembering was so hard. But if there *had* been sex with Josh, wouldn't she remember it? After all, sex with Josh would have to be unforgettable, no matter what you'd had to drink.

The next thing Heather managed to pull out of her aching brain was an image of Gaia Moore coming up to her and saying something terrible about Josh. Heather couldn't remember the exact words, but she knew it had been nonsense. Just another feeble Gaia move designed to screw up Heather's life. This time it wasn't going to happen. Gaia Moore had already stolen two boyfriends from Heather. Two was definitely enough.

Heather sat up in her chair and pushed her hair back from her face. Could Josh have given her something the night before that caused her to feel so bad in the morning?

Heather scowled. She shook her head swiftly, which made more `red-hot torture` swell up behind her eyes, but she didn't care. Josh was good. She knew it. He was gorgeous. He was funny. He was perfect. The only thing making her nervous was that Gaia had said all those ridiculous things to her. Heather wasn't about to let Gaia ruin her life. Not again.

To her surprise, the headache began to ease. *I'm seeing Josh tonight,* she thought. *No matter what Gaia says.*

Heather leaned back in her desk and watched numbly as the teacher wrote the list of characters on the board. All she had to do was sit through three more tedious hours of school, and then she could relax before her date. The thought took the edge off her pain.

Someone at the rear of the room laughed softly. Heather twisted in her seat to glance backward and saw Ed Fargo smiling in the last row. Next to him was Tatiana, her blond hair pulled back into a thick ponytail. She looked well put together in her black turtleneck sweater and camel-colored skirt. Unlike Gaia Moore, the Russian girl knew where to locate the shower and how to wear clothes that hadn't been stashed under the bed for a month.

While Heather watched, Tatiana leaned over to Ed and whispered something in his ear. Ed's smile turned into a laugh.

"Do you find Oedipus that hilarious, Mr. Fargo?" the teacher asked from the front of the room.

Ed shook his head. "Sorry, just thinking of. . ." His face tightened, and Heather could see that he was working hard not to laugh again. "Thinking of something else," he finished in a choked voice. Tatiana looked at him with mischief in her blue eyes.

Heather turned around in her seat. Before, seeing Ed flirt with Tatiana would have filled Heather with joy. After all, it had only been a couple of weeks since Gaia had taken away Heather's second chance with Ed. But now that Heather's new leaf had taken hold, she actually felt a pang of sympathy. From the way this girl was looking at Ed, it looked like tragedy had decided to take a break from Heather Gannis. It was Gaia's turn to lose Ed.

No wonder Gaia's losing it.

Another half-muffled laugh sounded from the back of the room.

Poor Gaia, thought Heather.

She was good with codes, probably as good as anybody outside of some **russian** crypto-nerds **curse** in the government, and she was still better than most of them.

TATIANA LEANED HER HEAD BACK

and drew in a deep breath. "I know that smell," she said.

Ed peeked at her over the top of a tall, narrow menu. "Tomato sauce and pepperoni?" He drew in a deep breath and closed his eyes. "*That* is the official smell of my dreams."

Pizza Ecstasy

The answer made Tatiana smile, but she shook her head. "Not that smell. The other smell." She searched her mind for the word. Her vocabulary was growing quickly, but this wasn't a term she had ever used in English before. "It's a black rock. You can burn it."

"You mean coal?" asked Ed.

"Yes, that's right. Coal." Tatiana took another breath and nodded. "They didn't use it around Moscow, not for heat, anyway, but in the summers my mother and I took several trips to the seashore. To the Black Sea, yes? In all the small towns we passed through, they still used coal for heating the houses." She tapped the side of her nose. "It smells the same in here as it did in those little towns."

"I don't think they heat this place with coal," said Ed, "but they do cook pizza with it. Lombardi's is the only place I know of with a coal oven." He frowned. "Does it smell too strong? Does it bother you?"

Tatiana wrinkled her nose. "It's not the best smell in

the world, but it's okay. It's like the smell of vacation. The smell you go past to get to the sea."

Ed put down his menu and folded his hands on the table. "Do you want to go back?" he asked.

For a moment Tatiana didn't understand. "To the Black Sea?"

"No," Ed replied with a shake of his head. "Or, yeah. If you want to, but I meant do you want to go home. Back to Russia."

"Oh. Of course. I have to go back."

"That's good because. . . because. . ." Ed's voice trailed off, and he looked at her with a blank expression. It took a few seconds for Tatiana to realize that Ed hadn't expected her to be so positive about returning to Russia.

"I'm sorry," she said. "New York is very exciting, but Russia is my home. Except for my mother, all my family is there. And all my friends." She paused for a moment and gave his hands a squeeze before letting them go. "Well, maybe not *all* my friends. Yes?"

"Yeah. I mean, I hope not." He flashed a smile. "You haven't even been to a Yankees game yet. How can you say you've even been to New York?"

Tatiana nodded. She took Ed's persistence as a good sign. Maybe he was beginning to let go of his feelings for Gaia. "I'll make sure that we make it to baseball season. Anyway, as long as they need my mother at work, we can't leave."

She studied him across the table. As usual, Ed's hair was unruly, but his face was good. Strong. He was handsomer than he thought he was, and Tatiana knew that this was a rare thing. Most boys who were good-looking knew they were good-looking. It didn't matter if they were in Russia or America. Maybe Ed had been more sure of himself once, before the accident, but Tatiana found that his modesty and kindness only made him more attractive. "I didn't know it mattered to you whether or not I stayed."

Ed's expression tightened. He opened his mouth, closed it again, then nodded. "Well, maybe you don't know as much as you think you do," he said at last.

Something a little more affirmative would have been the preferred response. Ed did want her to stay around; she could tell that. But maybe not for the reasons she was hoping for. There was something else. Something he didn't want to say. "And why would you want me to—"

Her question was interrupted as the waiter brought their pizza. Tatiana leaned back from the table as the waiter quickly put down plates. The pie was wide, with only a hint of crust at the edges and a molten sea of sauce and melted cheese in the middle. "Enjoy," the waiter said as he slipped the pizza onto a stone plate, flashed a smile, and strolled off to take another order.

Ed leaned over the food, closed his eyes again, and inhaled deeply. "Ahhh. Dreaming now." His mouth turned up in a smile that got wider by the minute. "It smells so good, I almost hate to eat it."

"That is okay. We don't have to—"

Ed's eyes popped open. "Oh, yes, we do." He grabbed up a slice and bit off the drooping point without bothering to put it on his plate. "Not eating this would be like. . . like having some great masterpiece and never looking at it."

"Like keeping a Picasso in your closet?" offered Tatiana.

"Worse." Ed took a larger bite and closed his eyes again in `pizza ecstasy`. "More like keeping a Zorlac Old School under your bed."

"Zorlac?"

"A very serious skateboard," said Ed. "Please don't compare it to a mere Picasso. We're talking serious classic. Just like this pie."

Tatiana took a piece of pizza and carefully removed it from the plate. She raised it toward her mouth, then paused and gave the slice a critical look. "It's burned."

"Nope," said Ed.

"It is black all over the bottom. I don't care what country you're in, black means burned."

"Try it."

"But—"

"Just try it!"

Tatiana was tempted to hold her nose, but she brought the slice to her mouth and took a small bite. At first she thought she'd been justified in thinking the food was ruined. The crust tasted sharp, smoky, bitter—burned. Then magic occurred on her tongue. The taste of the coal-smoked crust blended with the sweet tomato sauce and mellow cheese. Spices. Salty pepperoni. The combination was better than Tatiana would have believed. "It's very good," she said after swallowing the bite.

"Of course," Ed said. "Trust Lombardi's. Trust Ed. Have I ever lied to you?"

Tatiana smiled across the table at him and started to say something more, but there was a sudden twist in his expression that made her smile fade. "What?" she said. "Is something wrong, Ed?"

He shook his head. "No. It's only that a second ago, when you were frowning at your pizza, you looked a lot like—"

Until that moment the evening had been about the two of them. Now Tatiana felt a certain pesky third party creeping into the equation. "You thought that I looked like Gaia," she said. "That's what you were going to say. That's what you were going to say when we were walking last night, too."

Ed winced but nodded. "Yeah. Sorry."

Tatiana sat silently for a moment. "Is that why you want to hang around with me?" she said at last. "You can't be with Gaia, so you settle for me? Am I your substitute Gaia?"

This time Ed looked like he had been slapped. "No. Hell, no. I wouldn't do that."

Tatiana leaned back in her chair. She liked Ed. When her mother had first told Tatiana that they were coming to America, she had promised that Americans would be nice. That Tatiana would make new friends. That it would all be exciting and fun. But Tatiana had found New York a cold place. Not cold in temperature—Moscow won that contest easily—but coldhearted. The people didn't look at each other in the streets. The students at the Village School all seemed to have their own friends, and they showed little interest in making new ones. Until she'd met Ed, Tatiana had found the city a lonely, frightening place. Ed had been the first person to make her feel comfortable in her new home.

Ed was wonderful. He was funny. Helpful. He knew all the good secret places to go to. He was the perfect tour guide.

And was that all Tatiana wanted from him? A guide? If she wanted more, she was going to have to push past a large obstacle. A large, obnoxious obstacle that was sharing her mother's house.

"You and Gaia," she said calmly. "You had sex."

Ed's eyes went wide, and his face turned a color very close to the same shade as the tomato sauce. "Uhhh..."

"I think it was your first time," said Tatiana. She picked up her piece of pizza and nibbled off another cheesy bite.

For a moment Ed only stared at her with a blank expression. Then he shook his head. "It wasn't. I—"

"Your second time, maybe?"

Ed didn't reply.

Tatiana shrugged. "So, before you had sex, was Gaia as mean to you as she is now? Was she such a bitch?"

"Ummm. . ." Ed blinked a couple of times. "No." For a guy who was usually so quick with funny answers, Ed seemed to be having a hard time remembering how to operate his vocal cords.

"Did you date?"

"Not. . ." Ed picked up his glass and took a long swallow of soda. He sighed, drew in a breath, and tried again. "Not so much," he replied at last.

"So you just met and then had sex."

"Do people talk all the time like this in Russia? Is this a normal conversation?"

"Don't interrupt. What were you and Gaia like before you had sex?"

Ed rubbed a hand across his face. His skin was starting to return to a more normal color. "We were more like friends. We hung out together."

"Like you and me?" said Tatiana. "Like what we are doing tonight?"

"Yeah. I guess."

"And then you had sex."

"Tatiana!"

She laughed. "I'm only saying that sometimes sex is not as good as you think it will be. Especially when you don't have much practice."

"The sex was good!" Ed said loudly. "The sex was freaking great!" Several people from neighboring tables turned to look their way. A fresh coat of red came back to Ed's cheeks. He lowered his voice and leaned toward Tatiana. "Gaia and I didn't break up because of the sex."

"Then why did you break up?" Tatiana asked.

"I. . ." Ed paused, pulled in a deep breath, and shrugged. Still looking off into the shadows at the corner of the room, he went on in a voice that was little more than a whisper. "I don't know. I don't know what happened."

Tatiana studied his face in profile. She didn't know what had caused things to end between Ed and Gaia. She had her own ideas, of course. The worst idea was that things weren't ended at all. "You still want her." Ed only frowned in response and took another bite of pizza, but Tatiana went on. "It's all right. I know that you do. You can't change your feelings so quickly. After all, you are. . ." Tatiana waved a hand above the table. "What's the word I'm looking for?"

"In love?"

"No. An *idiot*."

Ed gave a sudden laugh that quickly turned to choking as he struggled to swallow a bite of pizza.

Tatiana waited until he recovered, then leaned across the table to bring her face closer to Ed's. "Gaia treats you like. . . like. . ." She tossed off a Russian curse and wished that her English were up to the level of swearing she needed. "She treats you so much worse than you should be treated. She really is a bitch."

"She's not," Ed said. Then he frowned. "Okay, so maybe she is. Sometimes. But she's not like that all the time. You don't really know her."

"Gaia is living in my house," said Tatiana. "I know how she treats my mother. I know how she treats me. I've seen how she treats you. From what I have seen, I don't think I want to know her any better."

"Gaia is different. Not like most people." From the tortured expression on his face, Tatiana could tell that Ed was also searching to find the right words. Even though they were speaking his language, Ed couldn't seem to explain how and why he loved Gaia Moore.

"Gaia is very pretty," said Tatiana. "I can see that. Is it only because she is so pretty that you like her?"

"No. It's—"

"But she is pretty."

"Of course, but—" Ed shook his head. "It's not like that. Gaia's. . . alive. Intense."

60

"I see," said Tatiana. She paused while the waiter came past and refilled their sodas. "I think I understand this now," she said when the man was gone.

"You do?" Ed gave a weak grin. "That's good. Maybe you can explain it to me."

Tatiana gave him back a smile of her own. "In Russia, I knew many girls who liked to date boys who were always in trouble. The handsome boys that wore black and frowned all the time. The boys that talked about crimes and how they'd hurt people. Even girls from good families do it."

"Bad-boy syndrome," said Ed. He put on a mock sneer. "The guys who might not be in gangs, but want you to think they are. They get a lot of girls here, too."

"And this is Gaia," said Tatiana.

"What?"

"I think you like Gaia because she is a bad girl. She is dangerous."

Ed shook his head sharply. "No, that's not right."

"I think it is." Tatiana sat back in her chair. She brought the straw to her lips and took a long sip of soda while she studied him across the table. "I think that Gaia is always in trouble. You're not. She's hard and mean to people. You're not. I think that you love Gaia because she is so much of what you're not. When you are with her, you feel dangerous. That's what makes her so exciting."

Ed's mouth dropped open, and he stared at her across the pizza. "That's not true."

"I think it's very true," said Tatiana. She picked up her slice of pizza and nibbled off another small bite. "I know it has been only a few days since you were with Gaia. You're too close to see the truth."

The expression on Ed's face still looked like shock. "I love Gaia," he said finally. "I don't know what else to say."

"Bad-girl syndrome. Think about it." Tatiana turned her attention to the pizza.

NOTE FROM TOM MOORE'S APARTMENT

(partially decoded by Gaia Moore)

TH# $#QU#N*# H%$ B##N !N$#RT#D %ND %LL T#$T$
!ND!*%T# TH# *@D# H%$ B##N !N*@RP@R%T#D !NT@ TH#
$UBJ#*T'$ @WN DN% $#QU#N*#.

T@ D%T# !ND!*%T!@N$ %R# TH%T TH# R#V!$#D *@D#
W!LL PR@DU*# TH# D#$!R#D R#$ULT$. TH# F!R$T
R#%*T!@N %PP#%R$ T@ B# T@T%LLY %B$#NT. *%R#FUL
M@N!T@R!NG W!LL B# R#QU!R#D T@ $## TH%T TH#
$UBJ#*T'$!N!T!%L *@D# D@#$ N@T R#%$$#RT !T$#LF
!N TH#$# #%RLY W##K$. H@W#V#R TH# *H%NG# $H@ULD
B# P#RM%N#NT.

!T !$ N@T P@$$!BL# T@ PR#D!*T %LL @TH#R #FF#*T$
TH# *@D# !N$#RT!@N M!GHT G#N#R%T#. TH#R# !$ %
P@$$!B!L!TY @F M#NT%L #FF#*T$. !MB%L%N*#. P$Y*H@$!$.
#V#N D#%TH.

TH# B#$T *@MPUT#R $!MUL%T!@N$!ND!*%T# TH%T
TH# $UBJ#*T W!LL #XP#R!#N*# %T L#%$T $@M# M#NT%L
DY$FUN*T!@N B#F@R# %G# TW#NTY.

<not legible>

RED-BROWN GREEN-BLUE BLUE-GREEN RED-BROWN
BROWN-RED GREEN-BLUE RED-BROWN GREEN-BLUE
BLUE-GREEN BROWN-RED BLUE-GREEN RED-BROWN
RED-BROWN BROWN-RED GREEN-BLUE BLUE-GREEN

GAIA OPENED HER EYES AND STARED

at the message. She was pretty sure she had enough to figure it out. She was good with codes, probably as good as anybody outside of some crypto- nerds in the government, and she was still better than most of them. Her first guess was that the message was in English. If that was so, then she could look at letter frequency, symbol-pair relationships, common phrases.

Hot Potato Gaia

She held the note up to the light. The letters that she had already decoded might or might not be correct, but it looked like some words were already jumping out of the text. *Subject.* That word was in there twice. *Symptoms.* That was near the bottom. If both of those were right, then—

Her thoughts were interrupted by a knock at the door.

"I'm busy," Gaia said. "Go away." If *symptoms* was right, then the first word was *two.* This was going to be easy.

"Gaia?" came Natasha's voice through the door. "Can I talk to you?"

"I said go away. Away." Gaia picked up her pencil and moved it across the page. This wasn't going to take minutes; it was going to be seconds. She could almost read the note right now.

The bedroom door opened, and Natasha walked in. Gaia spun around in her seat and stared at her. "I thought you were a translator. What part of 'go away' did you not understand?"

Natasha gave her a tight smile. The smile that Gaia thought of as the you're-a-worthless-little-snot-but-I-promised-your-father-I'd-look-after-you smile. "Do you really have to be so rude, Gaia?"

"Have to? No. But that doesn't mean I'm going to stop. Since you've apparently never heard of privacy, I'll pass on manners." She gathered up the papers from the top of the table and shoved them into a drawer.

"Really, Gaia," Natasha said with a sigh. "Tatiana and I are trying very hard to fit you into our life here."

Gaia swallowed sour laughter. "Sorry to be so inconvenient." It was clear that Tatiana was working very hard. Working very hard to steal the one guy that Gaia had ever made love to. Gaia had seen Tatiana flirting with Ed at school that afternoon. Flirting with Ed 101 seemed to be Tatiana's favorite subject.

Since school Tatiana hadn't made an appearance at the apartment, so Gaia figured the flirting was still in progress. Or maybe it was more than flirting now. Maybe Tatiana had already shown Ed what Gaia did wrong in bed. Maybe they were laughing about her right at that moment.

"Yeah, poor Tatiana," said Gaia. She ground her

teeth together so hard that she could hear the bones in her jaw squeaking.

Natasha tried to keep the smile on her face, but it was slipping quickly. She pulled out the chair in front of the dresser—a dresser that was covered with Tatiana's makeup and Tatiana's brushes and Tatiana's jewelry. She sat down with a tired sigh. "Gaia, I'm doing my best to help you. Why do you always want to make it so difficult?"

"Difficult?" Gaia pushed her hair back from her face and stared at Natasha. "Hey, I know! How about we drive down the street, pick out a house at random, and stuff you inside. While we're at it, maybe we should kill the people you care about most." She looked into Natasha's deep brown eyes. "What do you think? Maybe you could write me a note after you've been living with strangers for a year or two. I'm sure you'd be so happy because everybody is working so hard to be nice to you."

"We are not strangers," said Natasha. "Your father—"

"You *are* strangers. All of you. Even my father is a stranger." Gaia slapped her hand against the table with enough force to make the pencil she had been using jump and roll off onto the floor. "This is not a Hallmark special, and you're not my family."

"Your father loves you," Natasha said. Her voice was soft, and there was a hitch in her words, a rough-ness that surprised Gaia. "You are not the only one in this world who has lost someone, you know. You are not even the only one in this house. And you are not the only one who is away from the ones they care most about."

"I don't care about my father."

Natasha made a soft sound that might have been the ghost of a laugh. "You are not as good a liar as you think you are. You care. So does your father. He is doing what he thinks is best for you. And I. . ." She stopped and lowered her head into her hands. "I am very tired."

Gaia felt a momentary touch of sympathy. Natasha did look tired. Her skin was normally pale, but tonight she appeared almost ghostly. She looked smaller somehow, fragile. But none of that meant she could get away with telling Gaia what to do. Gaia was through being told what to do. "If you're tired of me," she said, "maybe I should leave."

"Yes," said Natasha, her voice muffled against her hands. "I think that might be for the best."

The words sent an unexpected shock running through Gaia. "You mean that?"

Natasha raised her head and nodded. Her face still looked drawn and exhausted, but her mouth was set in a firm, hard line that Gaia hadn't seen before. "I promised your father I would care for you, and I have tried. But I will not be the subject of endless abuse in my own home. I will not sit and watch you make my daughter miserable. I do not ask that you love us. I only ask for courtesy. If that's too much for you to give, I'll make arrangements for you to live elsewhere."

She stood up sharply, gave a quick nod, and turned to leave the room. Gaia was so stunned by the sudden turn in the conversation that she didn't even know how to start on a reply.

Natasha began to close the door, then stopped and turned back to Gaia. "Oh," she said. "I almost forgot. This came for you." She gave a flick of her wrist and sent an envelope looping across the room. "If you decide to move, you'll need to tell me where to send your mail." The door closed. The sound of Natasha's footsteps slowly receded down the hall.

For several seconds Gaia sat and looked at the closed door. *Did that really happen?* she wondered. *I just bought my freedom.*

She certainly wasn't going to let Natasha make "arrangements." It was bad enough having her father toss her to strangers. She wasn't going to let Natasha shove her farther down the line. Hot potato Gaia.

"I can go somewhere else," she said to the empty room. "There have to be options." A minute passed. Her set of options wasn't exactly longer than Santa's shopping list. She couldn't stay with Ed. Heather wouldn't exactly jump at the chance to have Gaia move in. There were some youth hostels downtown. Or maybe the classic bench in Central Park.

Finally Gaia got up and went to retrieve the envelope Natasha had tossed into the room so carelessly. She didn't expect much. It was probably some note from the school.

```
Dear Ms. Gaia's Keeper,
     Did you know the filthy beast has
been sleeping in class? Please poke
her with a sharp stick and keep her
awake so we can tell her many tedious
things she already knows.
                Your School Administration
```

But as soon as she picked it up, Gaia knew that this note hadn't been written by some clueless guidance counselor with a master's degree in how not to tell parents that their kids were hopelessly stupid. The envelope was made of gray paper. Pale gray paper with a crisp, linen texture. It was the same paper that had been used in the note that had led Gaia to her father's apartment.

She tore it open quickly and tipped the small note inside into her hand.

```
          Tonight. The Cloisters.
          Come at midnight.
```

AS SHE CAME THROUGH THE DOOR,

Heather was careful to keep smiling. The truth was, she hardly felt like smiling. More like mainlining a few hundred CCs of aspirin and sleeping for a week.

Unstoppable Urge

Even though the morning's monster headache was mostly gone, she couldn't remember ever feeling so tired, so worn down, so wrecked. But she kept smiling.

It wouldn't be good for Josh to see her looking sad or tired. Josh was beautiful. And Heather knew exactly how the game worked. The best-looking guys only went out with the best-looking girls. That was an absolute, unbreakable rule. You couldn't afford to let guys like that ever know that you were tired, or sick, or even sad. Good-looking guys, guys like Josh, they wanted only girls that were interesting and alive and always happy. Heather wasn't about to disappoint.

She bounced into the diner as if she had never felt better in her life. She scanned the tables for a moment and spotted Josh sitting at a booth toward the back. She flashed him a bright smile, gave a wave, and made her way through the crowded restaurant.

Josh slipped out of the booth and stood up as she approached. It seemed like an old-fashioned sort of thing to do, but he didn't stop there. He actually made a little bow and reached out to take her hand. "My lady," he said in a voice that dripped with a fake British accent. "You look particularly lovely tonight." He brought up her hand and touched it lightly to his lips. Then he let her fingers go and gave her a smile of his own. "Hey, how was school?"

"Terrible." Heather sat down and slid into the booth. "Horrible. The worst ever."

Josh dropped into the booth and frowned. "What went wrong?"

"You weren't there," said Heather.

Josh laughed. "I apologize for that. A terrible oversight on my part since it would have been a chance to spend more time with you." His smile faded a bit. "Hey, I need to apologize for crapping out on you last night."

Heather tried not to look as confused as she felt. Had Josh left her? It was just one of a million things she couldn't remember about the previous evening. "It's all right," she said, playing along. She didn't want Josh to pick up on the fact that she had no idea what he was referring to.

She felt a little more comfortable as they ordered their food. She laughed at Josh's jokes, and the last jabbing pains of her headache began to dull a bit. Josh asked more questions about school and the other students there. Heather filled him in, taking a few

71

shots at the stupidity of the teachers, the worthlessness of most of the students, how anxious she was to get out of high school and into college, where something really interesting might happen. She was relieved when their dinner finally arrived. She didn't have to be quite as entertaining while Josh downed a burger and fries.

After the food Heather began to feel tired again, and though she tried hard to fight it, the gaps in the conversation grew longer. She worked hard to think of something fresh to talk about, something provocative. And that's when Heather remembered Gaia Moore.

"Oh," she said. "Remember that girl Gaia I told you about?" She leaned forward and lowered her voice. "She says she knows you."

"Knows me?" Josh said with a raised eyebrow.

Heather nodded. "Yes. She says you're a dangerous man. Extremely dangerous. In fact, she says you're a killer." She waited for Josh to laugh, but to her surprise, the expression on his face was completely serious. Heather pressed her lips together, afraid that she had said something terribly wrong. "It's okay," she said. "It's only crazy Gaia. She's completely insane."

Josh looked at her. Looked down at his food. Then looked up again. The expression on his gorgeous face was unmistakably guilty.

Heather allowed herself to frown. "What? What's wrong?"

"I do know Gaia," said Josh.

"You. . . Gaia. . ." Heather stared at him in shock. "But you said you didn't."

"I know."

"You even made fun of her name."

Heather took a few seconds to concentrate on breathing. She had been so sure that everything Gaia told her about Josh had been a lie. Something Gaia had made up just to make Heather's life miserable. But if Gaia really did know Josh, then how much of what Gaia had said might be true? Heather couldn't remember all the things Gaia had said about him, but `cer-tain words wouldn't go away. Dangerous. Killer.`

Heather started to slide out of the booth, but Josh reached across the table and put a hand on her shoulder. "Wait," he said. "I'm sorry I lied. That was wrong. Completely wrong. Okay? I do know Gaia. It's just. . ." He gave a small, shy smile. "We were having such a good time. I didn't want Gaia messing up things between us before we even got started."

Heather pressed her lips together. "How do you know her?"

"Gaia and I knew each other a long time ago. We were. . ." He paused for a second, and his face took on an amused expression that Heather didn't like at all. "You might say our families were in business together. Gaia and I were friends and then, for a while, more than friends."

"You went out with Gaia?" Heather felt another surge of shock, but this time it was layered with extreme irritation. Wasn't there one guy in New York that Gaia Moore hadn't been with? Just one? Okay, it was easy to believe Gaia was a slut; maybe she went after every guy that moved. But shouldn't there be one guy in the entire city with actual taste? Why was it that every guy Heather ever liked had this fixation on a girl who looked like she hadn't washed her hair in a week and who had the fashion sense of a cockroach?

"It wasn't for long," Josh continued. "The thing with me and Gaia. We were together for a while, but it was bad news from the start. We've been split for a long time."

"She said you were a killer," said Heather.

"Oh, well, everybody knows that. Haven't you seen my picture in the post office?" Josh laughed. He took Heather's hand in his and gave her a reassuring glance. "Look, our little deal ended with some severe ugliness. I'm not surprised she's going around saying bad things about me." His smile got wide, and he rolled his eyes. "Though calling me a killer is pretty out there." He took his hand away from Heather's and leaned back against the padded leather of the booth. "I'm sorry she said all that crazy shit. I hope you didn't take it seriously."

"Of course not." Heather shrugged. "I mean, it's

Gaia, right? I know better than to take her seriously."

Josh smiled. "Good. Because that chick can get pretty dramatic. You should have heard some of the things she accused me of the day I broke up with her."

Suddenly the conversation was headed in a direction that Heather liked much, much better. "You dumped Gaia?"

"Yeah."

"She didn't leave you? You dumped her?"

"Uh-huh."

"When's the last time you saw her?"

"It's been a while," said Josh. "Maybe a year."

"And you don't want her back?"

"Want her back?" Josh seemed surprised. "Why would I want to be with Gaia when I'm with you?"

Heather let out a relieved breath. *He doesn't want her.* After another moment she became more excited. This was the way the world was supposed to be. For once, a guy had dumped Gaia and come to Heather. Okay, maybe it hadn't been a `straight dump-Gaia, beg-for-Heather deal`, but it was close. This was the first hint of justice Heather had seen since Gaia Moore had showed up at her school. The best-looking guy Heather had ever met had *dumped* Gaia Moore. There was still hope for the male of the species.

For a few seconds they were both silent. Then Josh put his hands on the table and stood. "Listen, I'm sorry, but I have to split," he said.

"Split?" Heather's chest tightened. "You're leaving? But we just finished eating. Don't you want to hang out for a little while?"

Heather couldn't believe she'd let herself say those words. Being vulnerable was against Gannis policy. Then again, so was getting plastered. Not to mention having sex in public places. Maybe Gaia wasn't the only one who was falling apart.

"I'm sorry, but I can't tonight," Josh replied.

Heather's vision blurred. Josh was leaving, and he didn't want her to go with him. Maybe he was already bored with her. Maybe he was even going to see Gaia. He had lied when he said he knew Gaia. Maybe he'd lied when he said he was over her. Maybe just hearing Gaia's name had stimulated some unstoppable urge to kiss those big puffy lips of hers.

Heather put her fingers to the bridge of her nose and squeezed. The Great Headache was making a return visit. "Why?" she said softly. "Why are you leaving?"

"It's something important." Josh reached out a hand to her. "Something that will change everything."

"Are you. . . . I mean, are we going to get together again?"

"Of course," said Josh. "This thing I'm doing tonight, it's not for me. It's for us."

"For us?" Heather blinked the forming tears away from her eyes. "What is it?"

"Will you trust me?"

Heather took his hand and gave her bravest smile. "I trust you."

Josh squeezed her hand and held it for a long, warm moment before letting go. He flashed another smile, dropped a twenty on the table without waiting for the bill, and hurried out into the dark streets.

Back in that never-never time
when I had parents, we used to
take vacations. Sounds like science fiction now, but it's one of
those things that real families
do. And no matter where we went,
we always rode on the subway.

· I'm not sure who it was that
was so into them. Maybe it was my
father. Maybe my mom. Maybe it
was me. That me from back then,
that me-with-a-mom, seems like
such a stranger now. I don't
always remember what that kid
liked.

I remember all those subways,
though. The one in Washington,
D.C., has these arched galleries
made from red stone and tracks
that cross over and under each
other in intersections that pile
up, one on top of another.

The one in London is really
old. I think maybe they built the
subway first, then sat back and
waited until the city settled
over it. In some parts you get on
subway cars that look pretty

normal. In other parts you get on these weird little cars with curved tops that seem like definite Sherlock Holmes territory. And they're made out of this ancient tile that gives everything this strange, hollow echo.

But the thing I remember most about the London Underground is "the gap." I'm not talking about the overpriced McDonald's-of-clothes kind of Gap. This gap is the space between the edge of the platform and the door of the subway car. It's not all that big, but in London they warn you—repeatedly—to mind it. There's this endless mechanical voice that says "mind the gap" over and over whenever the doors open and shut.

When we were on vacation there, my mom started using the phrase "mind the gap" all the time instead of "be careful." She continued to use it after the vacation had ended, too, and I started saying it back.

"Mind the gap going to school today, Gaia."

"Okay, Mom. You mind the gap, too." It was a ritual thing. You know, step on a crack, you break your mother's back. Remember to say "mind the gap," and your mom is safe for the day.

Sometimes when I'm on the subway in New York, I think about the gap. I almost expect to hear that robo-voice with the British accent saying the words over and over. Mind the gap. Mind the gap. It's pretty good advice for people riding the subway. There are plenty of gaps down there. And not just the kind you might step into.

Guys with shaved heads and big knives. Guys with drugs. Guys with guns. Those are some pretty common gaps.

In the daytime it's crowded but usually calm. Ninety percent people on their way to work. Nine percent tourists. One percent assorted New York City weirdness.

But nighttime is a completely different story. The night shift is more like ninety percent

weirdness, nine percent working,
and one percent Oh My God, Did
You See That. Lots of gaps.

But I guess you don't have to
be on the subway to find a gap.
My mom told me to mind the gap
the day she died. I'm not sure I
said it back. I think so, but
some six-year-old part of my
brain says I didn't. Because if I
did, my mom would have been safe.

She wouldn't have been swal
lowed by the gap.

Gaia walked
slowly,
looking for
her
unknown
partner in
this
midnight
blind date.

enemy

team

GAIA GOT OFF THE SEVENTH AVENUE

Ignorance Is Bliss

subway line and climbed the steps up to the street. It was late, and the air had cooled at least twenty degrees while she had been underground. She took a moment to get her bearings, then plunged across the street and headed for Fort Tryon Park.

The Cloisters was hidden in the middle of little Fort Tryon Park. Any park was probably not on the list of most recommended places to visit in New York after midnight. But since Gaia had recently been spending her nights stalking around Central Park and had spent countless evenings flushing muggers out of Washington Square Park, this didn't seem like a big deal. Even if she had been capable of feeling fear, Fort Tryon Park probably wouldn't have rated a scare. The whole thing was only less than a mile wide.

But if the place for this meeting wasn't anything to get excited about, the person she was meeting might be. Gaia had no idea who had written the note. It could have been Loki or someone in Loki's organization. Someone like Josh. Gaia knew that Josh was in town, and Josh knew that Gaia had seen him. This whole thing with the notes and the meeting might be a trap. But it might not. The note could have come from Gaia's father. Though why would her father have written a note that explained how to find his own apartment unless he had planned to meet her there? No, it was almost certainly an enemy.

That was a good guess because Gaia seemed to have such a constantly growing list of enemies, while her list of friends got smaller every day. Sam was dead. Mary was dead. The fragile friendship she had thought was starting with Heather was broken. Even Ed was gone. She had pushed him away—to keep him safe— and it looked like he was going to run right into the skinny arms of Tatiana. The two of them probably spent all night telling Gaia's Most Embarrassing Moments stories to each other.

The enemy team was definitely winning the recruitment drive.

Gaia shook her head. She was almost there. A few more minutes and she would know who was behind the gray notes.

She jogged across a street through light traffic. New York might be the city that never sleeps, but the neighborhood around Fort Tryon Park was definitely taking a power nap. There was no one on the sidewalks, and only a few lights were on in the nearest apartment buildings. As Gaia slid in between the trunks of the huge old oaks at the park's perimeter, an odd hush fell around her. The park might be small, but the trees did a great job of blocking the sounds and lights of the city.

Like the surrounding neighborhood, the park was very serene. Lighting was sparse. Gaia found herself walking from one small pool of light, through wide areas of darkness, and into another temporary patch of brightness. It was too cold for crickets or frogs, though something small could be heard moving in the bushes. A wind kicked up, rattling the few dry leaves that remained on the trees. The moon rose up over the buildings to the east and added a pale pewter glow to the shadows.

"All right," she said to the darkness. "You can stop trying to scare me. Won't work. Wish it would, but it won't." Only she did feel something, a weird tingling at the center of her chest. Was this a last little touch from her uncle's amazing Technicolor psycho serum, or was being creeped out a different emotion from fear?

A few steps later she came up a slight rise and saw the Cloisters ahead. The Hudson River shone through the trees behind the building, its surface rippled with moonlight. The building itself seemed like something that had been lifted right out of medieval Europe and dropped on New York. An alien visitor sneaking in on the city from another time. Another world. In the moonlight the building was all strange angles and dark pools of shadow. Roman columns. Gothic arches.

Bas-relief statues too dim to make out in the faint light.

Gaia walked slowly, looking for her unknown partner in this midnight blind date. There was no sign of anyone waiting outside the building, so Gaia made a slow circle until she found a way through a covered arcade to the interior. The incredible unbroken quiet continued as she passed through a row of smooth pillars, across a pitch black walkway, and past more pillars into a moonlit central plaza.

Waiting for her in the center of the open space was a tall, solid figure in a trench coat. There was a fedora hat on the stranger's head and shadows across his face.

Her father? Gaia took a half step forward. No, the shape was wrong. Tall, but not quite tall enough. Too thick. Not Loki, either. "All right," she said to the stranger. "I'm here. What do you want?"

The figure raised his head, and moonlight fell across the features of a wide, weathered face. "Gaia?"

Gaia blinked and stared in surprise. "George?"

A moment later, before any part of her brain that had anything to do with thinking could even start to kick in, she was hugging him. Life in the Niven household had been unpleasant, to be sure, but compared to what had come after, those days in the brownstone now seemed like a fairy tale. At least then she'd had Sam. And Mary. And Ed. . .

When she realized that she was still hugging the retired agent, Gaia stepped back. "Um, yeah. Sorry," she said. "I didn't expect it to be you. I figured more, somebody looking to put new holes in my head."

George smiled at her, his big teeth visible even in the poor light. "It's all okay," he said. "I don't mind."

"What are you doing here?" asked Gaia. "Did you send the note?"

"Yes," George said with a nod.

"And the first note?"

"I've been worried about you," he said. "I wish you had never gone off on your own."

Gaia was suddenly very glad it was dark. That way George couldn't see how badly she was blushing. "I thought, you know, after Ella. . ."

George turned away from her, his face once again hidden by shadows. "I don't understand all the actions of my wife. I guess I never will."

"She ended up saving me," said Gaia.

"Yes, that's the important thing. The thing I have to remember." He continued to look off into the darkness, his expression unreadable. "Everything else Ella did, well, it's over now. But she did save you."

"She did." Gaia took a step to the side, hoping to get a better look at his face. "Why did you send me the note?"

"I wanted to meet you."

"Not this note. The first one. The note that told me how to find the apartment."

"Ah." Finally George turned back to her, though his face was still hard to see clearly in the pale moonlight. "I had hoped your father would be there to meet you, but soon after I sent the note, I learned he had abandoned the apartment. Still, I thought that if you went there, you might find some evidence."

"Evidence of what?" asked Gaia.

George didn't reply for a moment, though Gaia could hear him pull in and release a long breath. "Gaia, I think your father is being betrayed."

"By my uncle?" asked Gaia. "I already know about—"

"Not your uncle." George took a step toward her. His long coat left a trail in the dew-soaked grass. "The conflict between your father and uncle is an old one. Who can even say which one of them is right?"

I can, thought Gaia. *The one that shot my mother? Not right.*

George shoved his hands into the pockets of his coat. "There's someone else. Someone that's become very close to him." He paused for a second. "Did you get into the apartment?"

"Yeah," said Gaia. She thought about the climb up the outside of the building. Even without fear, it now seemed to her more than a little crazy. It also seemed like something that George definitely did not need to know about. "It took some work, but I got in."

"What did you find?"

Gaia shrugged. "Nothing. Someone had been there before me. Did some serious redecorating. That classic slice-open-the-couches-and-tear-up-the-books style."

"Damn," George said under his breath. "Then there's no proof."

"Proof of what?" Gaia blinked and tried to stare through the darkness. "Who's after my father this time?"

Instead of answering, the retired agent only stood, head down and hands in pockets, his shoulders drooping. "Gaia," he said in a tired tone. "Why don't you come back and stay with me?"

The offer was tempting. Almost too perfect. Natasha had just done the shape-up-or-ship-out routine. Gaia's other living arrangements seemed to be limited to cardboard boxes. Plus staying with George would mean not having to share space with Tatiana. Not having to watch as Tatiana methodically reeled Ed in. Not watching Ed get torn away from her like everyone else she had ever cared about. All good points.

"Who's after my father?" she asked.

George sighed. His skin seemed to sag on his face. "It's a shame he doesn't tell you these things himself." George shook his head, his fedora bobbing in the moonlight. "I've never understood why he treats you the way he does."

"Look, sometimes I don't understand him, either, but that's not really the point right now." Gaia was anxious for George to get on with it. "Can you just tell me who's after him now?"

The agent took another deep breath. "I don't know."

"What?" Gaia felt a spark of anger. "But you just said that—"

George pulled his hands from his pockets and held them up in front of Gaia. "I know there's a traitor. Information on your father is leaking from somewhere. His secrets are starting to be known in the intelligence channels. I think that someone close to your father is actually a spy for Loki."

"What secrets?"

"Those are things you need to discuss with him." He dropped his arms to his sides. "Please, Gaia, for your own safety. Come back where I can keep an eye on you."

Gaia considered it for a second. But she couldn't bear the thought of going back to that house. Too many ghosts. Besides, knowing as little as she did about the situation, she couldn't be sure it was the right decision. "Not now," she said. "Not until you tell me more about what's going on."

George shook his head. "I've told you all I can for now. Anything more would only be increasing your danger."

Anger and frustration flared again. "Well, I can't move in with you until I have more information."

"It's your decision, but I'm only looking out for your best interests," said George. He stood up straighter, and suddenly Gaia could see the agent in the gray-haired, overweight man. "Gaia, I have more than thirty years' experience with the intelligence business. Have a little faith that I know what I'm talking about."

Gaia nodded, but she still wasn't big on the ignorance-is-bliss theory. She wanted to know the answers, not be protected from them. "When will you tell me what's really going on?"

George rubbed at his chin. "When I learn more, I'll tell you. I'll be in touch."

"Good," said Gaia.

Unexpectedly George held out his hand. "Gaia, we need each other now," he said. "We need to work together to stop whoever it is that's after your father." With that, he let go of her hand. Then he turned and walked away into the moonlight.

THREE HOURS OF STANDING AROUND

had made Tom stiff, tired, and bored. He'd been staking out The Rip, a tiny, windowless

Tough Guy

bar that sat off at one end of town along a strip of bluff too high and stony to make for a good hotel spot. The building was low and made from unpainted concrete blocks. There was only a door in the front, a door in the back, a hand-painted sign, and lots of gray concrete. It was the kind of place where locals went for serious drinking and where not-so-locals went for serious business. Every now and then some tourists would drop by, looking for a little island color. But they never tried it twice.

Early in the evening the place had been almost deserted, but as the night got longer, the crowd got bigger. The tiny parking lot filled up with a strange mix of rusted-out Chevrolets and brand-new Mercedes. More customers arrived on foot or on bicycles that they left leaning against the concrete walls. Tom could well imagine the kinds of deals that were being made inside the small building. There would be smugglers working out routes to bring goods past customs or to ferry people around immigration. Drug dealers would be making arrangements to handle cocaine from Central America. There might even be some modern-day pirates working out targets among the fancy yachts that were anchored offshore. None of that business concerned Tom. Not tonight.

Tonight was earmarked for finding the so-called Noel. But Tom was beginning to think that the guy with the speargun had sent him to the wrong place.

He was ready to go back to his small hotel on the south end of the island and wait out another tedious day without getting a step closer to Loki.

Could coming to the Caymans have been a mistake? It had seemed so important at the time. Loki was doing something here, something that required a lot of his funds and a large number of his operatives to be moved to this tropical oasis. Coming down to investigate had seemed essential. But after spending days chasing shadows around the islands, Tom wished he had stayed in New York. If he had stayed, at least he would be close to Gaia. And to Natasha. Tom gave a quick, silent prayer that the two of them were getting along. If Gaia would only give Natasha half a chance, he was sure that they would get along great. On the other hand, his daughter had reason not to rely on random acts of kindness.

Headlights appeared on the narrow strip of blacktop that separated The Rip from the more modern buildings of Red Bay. Tom held himself tight against a palm tree as the lights moved past his hiding place and on to the parking lot. The car was a little Mazda Miata. Black, shiny, and new.

Out of the tiny car stepped a woman so tall that Tom had to wonder how she ever fit inside. She was at least six-foot-two. Broad shouldered. Short-cropped hair dyed a screaming orange-red, and she wore a sleeveless blouse so sheer that even the moonlight shone straight through. She gave herself a quick once-over in the side-view mirror of her car, then headed into The Rip with a long, purposeful stride.

Tom waited in the trees a few minutes longer. The quarter moon was standing well above the waves, turning the ocean black and silver. A breeze began to send the palm trees swaying and drove away the warmth of the day.

He had a very bad feeling about this. Tom reached into his pocket and touched the cool metal weight of the small .32-caliber revolver. He knew that this woman was part of Loki's organization, and she was his only lead to what Loki was doing down here in the islands. Just getting her name had taken him the better part of a week. There was no choice except to go after her. But Tom had no illusions. Whatever happened inside this little bar, it wasn't going to go down clean and it wasn't going to be easy.

Broken seashells crunched under his feet along the path to the entrance. There was no door really, only a door-sized hole with nothing at all to stop anyone from moving in and out. A small sign taped to the concrete indicated the bar had rated an *A* from the department of health. Tom wondered for a moment how large a bribe it had taken to earn that *A*.

Inside, the windowless room was almost completely dark. There were a few lights behind the bar itself, enough that the bartender could tell whiskey from rum. Some of the men turned to look as Tom stepped in between the clusters of small tables. Most didn't bother.

It took a few seconds for Tom's eyes to adjust to the room well enough to let him navigate between the irregular rows of tables and past the knots of standing men. He did one quick sweep of the place, stopped near the back wall, and turned around. The woman wasn't there. Another look around the room showed that there was another open door to the outside at the back and a third door on the left. Unlike the empty frames leading out, this last door was made of wood and was solidly closed. Unless the woman had walked straight through the front of the bar and right out the back—which was entirely possible—she had to be behind the door.

Tom walked across the room and reached for the doorknob. Before he could touch it, there was a soft click from behind his head. He turned and saw a barrel-chested man in a yellowed T-shirt. In the man's hand was a gun so small, it almost looked like a toy.

"Hey, my friend," the man said. "You don't have any business in there."

"I'm here to see a woman named Noel."

"Everybody loves our Noel. Right now she's busy, and I don't think. . . I don't. . ." The gun came down a couple of inches. "Hey, don't I know you?"

Tom turned slightly so he could get a better look at the man. The guy was short, but he was wide across the shoulders and thick in the arms. A tough guy. A guy that was used to pushing people around and getting his own way. Only there was a look of fear on this tough guy's face. Tom took a guess about what was making the man afraid and decided to go with it.

"That's right," he said. "I think you do know me. I'm called Loki."

The man's eyes opened so wide, it was a wonder they didn't fall from his head. Immediately the gun came down. "Sorry, sir. Mr. Loki. Sir. I, uh, I didn't recognize you at first. I mean, I only saw you the one time and that was from a long way off, and I never expected to see you here, so I—"

"That's all right," said Tom. "I take it you have no objection if I go on inside?"

"Of course not, sir!" said the man in the T-shirt. "I'll stay right out here and watch the door."

Tom smiled at him. "It's good to have such well-trained associates." He gave the man a final nod. Then he grabbed the doorknob, pulled it open, and stepped inside.

The room was small. There was a round card table with the surface covered in stained green felt. Around the table were four chairs. Three of them were already occupied. The woman, Noel, sat on the opposite side, facing the door. Though the light in the room was far from bright, she wore a pair of pink-tinted sunglasses. On her left was a thin, dark-skinned man with a neat, sharply creased dress shirt and a pencil-thin mustache. On her right was the man who had been carrying the speargun on the beach.

All three of them turned toward the door as Tom entered. The reactions were quite different. The woman looked at Tom curiously but said nothing. The man with the thin mustache stood up quickly, his arms at his sides. He had the look of someone that had recently been released from the military and was used to jumping to attention every time an officer entered the room.

"Good evening, sir!" he barked.

The man from the beach also stood. He took two quick steps back, his eyes never leaving Tom, until he was pressed against the concrete wall of the bar. There was a wide series of bandages running across his broken nose, but the eyes above it showed a mixture of fear and hate. "That's the man who attacked me!"

"Really," said the woman. Her voice was cool. "That's interesting."

"He nearly killed me."

The man with the mustache gave a short bark of laughter. "Shut up," he said. He made a sharp nod toward Tom. "This is Loki."

Broken Nose stared at Tom again. Now his primary emotion was simple confusion. "If he's Loki, then why did he attack me?"

"Maybe because you're an idiot?" said the other man.

"This man is not Loki," Noel explained.

It was the mustache man's turn to be afraid. He looked at Tom again, and his right hand crept closer to a bulge under his shirt. "Then who is he?"

The woman tilted her head. "I don't know. But it should be interesting to find out." She pulled out a lighter from somewhere below the table, lit a thin, black cigarillo, and placed it between her lips. "Are you coming over here to join us?"

Tom took another step into the room. "I'm only looking for some information. Once I get it, I'll be quite happy to leave you to enjoy the rest of the evening."

"Information," the woman repeated. She let out a long streamer of blue smoke. "Seems to me that you're more interested in trouble."

"The information will be enough," said Tom. "You can keep the trouble."

"We'll see," said the woman. She blew out more smoke and looked at Tom through the cloud. "What is it that you want?"

Tom took the back of the last chair, twisted it around, and sat with his legs straddling the chair and the wooden back against his chest. He studied the thugs for a moment. Broken Nose had a German accent. The mustache man had something of a Cuban look. Noel. Noel he couldn't place at all. Tom wondered briefly about the background of these three, but it didn't really matter. Only one thing mattered tonight. "I'm looking for someone."

"For Loki."

"That's right."

The woman studied him for a few minutes, her eyes like red coins behind the tinted glasses. "You are twins."

"Something like that," said Tom. "So, why don't you help out a wayward relation and tell me where to find him?"

It took the woman two long pulls and two slow exhales of smoke before she answered. "Why don't you share a little information with me? Once I know some more about you, maybe I'll be willing to share."

"What do you want to know?"

"We could start with your name." It was a simple enough question, but as the woman asked it, she was no longer looking at Tom. She was looking over his right shoulder.

Tom didn't make an attempt to answer. Instead he kicked hard to his left, tipping over his chair, coming down on one shoulder and coming up with the wooden chair in his hands. A gunshot snapped past the side of his head, and he felt and splinters fly from the surface of the table.

The man with the mustache was on his feet. Behind him the broad-shouldered man in the T-shirt was starting into the room, his gun drawn. The woman was up. Broken Nose was moving. Everybody was moving.

A knife came from Tom's left. He swung the chair hard against a skull. The chair broke into a dozen pieces. Mustache fell like a sack of potatoes. Tom dropped and took down T-shirt with a sweep of his leg. He then tucked and rolled as another gunshot chipped at the ancient floor tiles. Back on his feet, Tom put a stiff hand into Broken Nose's gut and a fist into the already injured face. Broken Nose screamed. Then he went down and stayed down. All three men were out of the picture. That only left. . .

A blow struck Tom in the side with such force that it spun him around and sent him staggering against the concrete wall. He shook off the effect and turned toward the woman.

Despite everything, the little black cigarillo was still in Noel's mouth and a faint smile was on her lips. "You not only look like him," she said. "You fight like him."

"I hope not," said Tom. He came at her in a crouch. Aimed a kick toward her thigh.

The red-eyed woman blocked, countering with an

elbow that sent Tom's breath burning back up his throat.

He avoided a follow-up blow, put a fist into her side, and drew back to the other side of the scarred card table.

It wasn't until an incredible pain bloomed on Tom's left arm that he realized that (1) the woman had a pistol, (2) she was shooting at him, and (3) he was hit.

Before a second shot could find him, Tom grabbed the edge of the round table and flipped it toward the woman. Bullets punched through the tabletop, showering Tom with splinters, but he rushed forward, pinning the woman against the wall. There was a satisfying grunt as she struck the concrete, followed by the clatter of the gun striking the floor. The woman scrambled free and made a dive for the gun. Tom kicked it away. He aimed a second kick toward her, but she grabbed his foot and gave his leg a painful twist that forced Tom to stagger back.

He winced as he watched the woman climb to her feet and turn to face him. *Twenty years ago,* he thought, *this would have been over in a second.* But it wasn't twenty years ago, and the warmth spreading along Tom's arm meant that blood was flowing from his wound. He had to end this soon.

The woman went on the attack, launching a quick series of kicks, jabs, more kicks. It was all Tom could do to stay on his feet. He circled left, protecting his injured arm. He was breathing very hard now, and his arm was throbbing. The woman darted in again. This time Tom struck back. He landed a quick, sharp fist to the woman's chin, then spun and laid a roundhouse kick that caught her high up on the right leg. The woman fell.

Tom was on her before she had a chance to recover. He pinned her legs beneath his weight and held her down with a forearm against her windpipe. "Tell me where he is," he said.

The rose-colored glasses had been lost in the fight. The woman's eyes were now a very ordinary light brown. "He'll kill me if he finds out I told," she choked out from beneath Tom's grip.

"Maybe." Tom pressed down harder. "But if you don't tell, I'll kill you right now."

The woman's face turned an alarming shade of purple before she finally nodded. "McHenry."

"What is that? A town?"

"Medical. . . school. McHenry. . . Medical. . . School."

"Thanks," said Tom. "If you're lying, I'll be back to ask you again. Only next time I won't be so polite." Then he doubled the pressure on the woman's throat.

Her brown eyes bulged, and she bucked against him wildly. But only for a moment. When she stopped moving, Tom checked her pulse. It was still there, still strong. There was blood on her blouse, but as far as Tom could tell, it was his.

He stood up and looked around the room. Three men and one woman lay unconscious on the floor. *I should kill them,* he thought. *As soon as I'm gone, they'll be hurrying off to tell Loki that I was here.*

He had no doubt that if the roles were reversed, that if it were Loki who needed to protect himself, the deaths of four people wouldn't even cause him to think twice.

It wasn't that way for Tom. He looked down at his bloody hands. He paused for a moment and wiped his palms against the broken remnants of the green card table. Then he headed for the door.

It was time to go to school.

Guide to Offshore Institutions, 14th Edition

McHenry Medical College
Cayman Islands
14 Sea Bee Road

Overview

McHenry is considered one of the best institutions in the southern Caribbean. It has more modern equipment than most such schools, and the teacher-to-student ratio is unusually adequate. Unlike some institutions, McHenry has met with moderate success in finding stateside residencies for its graduates. The school has some reputation in cytology and genetics, with several notable research grants being awarded throughout the last decade.

McHenry closed its doors in 1999 for remodeling. However, the college spokesperson insists that the school is still in business and will reopen with the newest, most up-to-date instruction and facilities possible for the 2002 fall semester.

Enrollment

YEAR	STUDENTS
1995	113
1996	121
1997	130
1998	130
1999	0

If you ever get to the point where you don't like breakfast food, you are one poor excuse for a human being. All the best junk comes at breakfast. Doesn't matter if you're going for your high-end eggs Benedict or your basic brown sugar cinnamon Pop-Tart—it's all good.

Consider this amazing but true fact: Breakfast is the only meal of the day where a doughnut counts as the main course.

Think about the sheer variety of breakfast goodness. Giant-size biscuits loaded with sausage and eggs. Put them in a sack, and it's rendered transparent from all the oil by the time you leave the counter. That's how you know it's good. Bear claws. Pancakes with syrup. Western omelettes. Cereals made from ninety-five percent real sugar and five percent artificial color. Who wouldn't want to eat this stuff?

I think breakfast is more of a guy meal. From what I've seen, girls like dinner. They like a

meal that requires them to be
seated and comes off nice plates.
Salad. That's a girl food.
Anything French? Automatically
way over on the female side.
Except maybe for the fries. And
the toast. Left to themselves,
most guys honestly prefer food
that comes out of styrofoam pack-
ages and where the only decision
on protocol is whether to dunk
the hash browns in ketchup or
just scarf them straight from the
bag. There are very few girl
foods at breakfast.

There are, of course, exceptions
to these strict gender lines. I've
also seen the girl risk life and
limb—literally—for a Krispy Kreme.
An attitude that seems perfectly
reasonable to any guy.

I'm not saying that her guy-
like breakfast attitude is what
makes Gaia attractive. The whole
so-beautiful-you-think-you-might-
die-just-from-looking-at-her
thing helps with that. The breakfast food appreciation is a
bonus. Another part of the whole

big Mystery That Is Gaia.

In my case, that might be more Misery than Mystery. The Misery Of *Not* Being With Gaia. Not getting to watch her pull the last slivers of cheese from a McMuffin wrapper. Not witnessing her scrape the last drops of chocolate and stray jimmies from a doughnut box using nothing but her tongue. It's painful.

Of course, there's a simple reason for the pain. Gaia hates me.

Okay, maybe that's putting it too simply. Gaia can't stand to look at my ugly face and wouldn't be with me for all the Krispy Kremes in New York. There. I think that's closer to the truth.

The Gaia-hates-me thing seems pretty clear. It's the *why* of it that keeps me beating my head against the wall. Gaia was with me. Then she wasn't. And I don't know why.

Any guy with anything that even remotely resembled a brain would drop this mess and get together with Tatiana. Tatiana is beautiful. A knockout. She's not beautiful in

the same way that Gaia is beautiful, but that doesn't mean she's
less beautiful. Like Gwyneth
Paltrow is beautiful, but so is
Jennifer Aniston. Beautiful, but
very different.

And not only is Tatiana easy
on the eyes, she's also smart.
She's got talent. Her drawings
are amazing. And then there's the
real bonus: She likes me. How
often does that happen? Exotic
beauty from the other side of the
planet comes to New York and
homes in on Ed Fargo. Trust me,
this is not an everyday event.

Only I don't think Tatiana would
ever be caught dead licking cheese
off a McDonald's wrapper or shoving
down a bucket of The Colonel's
chicken. No matter how beautiful
she is, no matter how much she
likes me, Tatiana eats three well-
rounded meals a day, using silver-
ware. Tatiana is not Gaia.

And Gaia is still what I want.
Breakfast, lunch, and twenty-four
hours a day.

Ed looked at
her and felt
a little
nervous.
Heather's
pilot light
definitely
seemed to
be burning
low.

a
nice
hard
shot

ED PUSHED HIS POTATOES FROM ONE

side of the plate to the other, then pushed them back again. They were genuine American fries. Prepared as only a diner could make them. Crispy at the edges, soft in the middle, and guaranteed to contain enough grease to lube a four-speed

Burning Low

transmission. So why couldn't he work up an appetite to eat them? He scowled down at the brown fries. Any girl who could keep him from enjoying a plate of potatoes and grease was a girl to be avoided.

A cold breeze ran through the diner as a handful of breakfast latecomers slipped inside. Ed glanced at them, looked back at his food, then raised his head again. In the group of people milling around the counter was a face that Ed didn't expect to see in such a bright, early, and artery-clogging situation. Heather Gannis.

Ed raised a hand and started to call her over, then he hesitated. Was it really Heather? The face looked basically right, only this girl had sunken cheeks and dark circles under her eyes. Heather's hair usually looked as though she were ready to do a shampoo commercial. Swirl left, swirl right, big shower of Chestnut Brown Number 37. But this girl had hair that was definitely on the "before" side of any before-and-after ad.

It wasn't until the girl turned toward Ed and gave a weak smile that he was absolutely sure it was Heather. He waved. "Hey," he said. "Looking for a seat?"

Heather dropped her purse onto the table and sat down on the chair across from Ed. "Morning," she mumbled. Her eyes were half closed. She opened them long enough to glance at Ed, then let them close again.

Ed wasn't sure what to say. He understood that no girl was ever prepared to hear, "Wow, you know, you look like total crap," as constructive criticism, but that was certainly what Ed wanted to say. Not only did Heather look like death—she also looked *wrong.* While he was no expert, he was pretty sure that her striped green-and-yellow pants did not go with her fuzzy red sweater. And her hair wasn't just flat—it was uncombed. The whole situation gave Ed a bad feeling. It was as if the zero-fashion-sense spirit of Gaia Moore had taken over the totally style-driven body of Heather Gannis. From the look on Heather's face, the transplant wasn't going too well.

"Are you hungry?" Ed asked. He couldn't remember Heather ever eating the diner's grease-drenched breakfast fare, but she sure looked like she needed something.

Heather shook her head, her eyes still half closed. "I only came in for some coffee."

Ed managed to wave down a waitress and get

Heather a cup of steaming black coffee. Without pausing to add any milk or sugar, Heather snatched the cup in both hands and took a long gulp. Ed half expected her to scream—the diner kept their coffeepot at a temperature that Ed estimated to equal that of the surface of the sun—but Heather only paused long enough to take a breath, then went back to swallowing coffee. Finally, when the cup was nearly empty, she opened her eyes and looked down at the chipped mug with a scowl.

"This stuff is terrible."

"Then why are you drinking it?" asked Ed.

Heather stared at the empty cup. "I need something to get me going."

"I thought you were more of a caffé latte type," said Ed. "Don't you usually do your coffee consumption over at Starbucks?"

Heather lifted the cup and slid the last of the coffee into her throat. "I needed something stronger this morning. Besides." She paused and wrinkled her nose. "All my friends are over there, and I don't really want to deal with them this morning."

"I understand," said Ed. He gave his cold potatoes another shove across the plate. "Glad I'm not one of those friends of yours."

"Oh, no, Ed." Heather put down her cup and levered her tired eyes open to look at him. "You know you're my friend. You're more important to me than, well, than any of those people down at Starbucks."

Ed was almost as surprised as he had been by Heather's appearance. Since he had gotten together with Gaia, there hadn't been many warm and tender moments with Heather. And since he had broken up with Gaia, there hadn't been many moments with Heather at all. Ed wondered what other expressions of love would come from this Strange Bizzaro Heather. "Are you sure you're okay?"

Heather nodded. She held up her cup to catch a refill of coffee, then downed half the cup in another gulp. "Yeah, I'll be fine." She stifled a yawn. "Just fine."

"Okay," said Ed. "Good to hear it."

Heather suddenly smiled. "Did I tell you about the guy I'm dating?"

"Coffee-in-the-lap guy?" asked Ed.

"How'd you know?"

"We talked about him in the cafeteria the other day, remember?"

"Oh, right." Heather chuckled and rolled her blue eyes.

"So, how many times have you gone out with this guy, anyway?"

Heather looked off into space. "Three. Or is it four?"

Ed looked at her and felt a little nervous. Heather's pilot light definitely seemed to be burning low. He glanced at his watch and tossed a buck onto the table. "Look, I need to get to school. You coming?"

"Huh?"

"To. School," Ed said slowly. "You. Come?"

"Not right now," said Heather. She took another swig of coffee. "I'll be there later."

Skipping class wasn't exactly normal Heatherness, but in Bizarro Land. . .

"Sure," said Ed. "I'll see you there." He pushed himself up onto his crutches and wove through the crowd to the door. Once he reached the sidewalk, Ed paused and looked back through the glass. Heather was still sitting there, the coffee cup clutched in both hands. Once Heather had been his girlfriend. Then after the accident they broke up but stayed pretty close. At times Ed had thought of Heather as his closest friend. But the pale Heather Gannis in there drinking coffee seemed like a stranger.

IT TOOK FOUR CUPS OF THE AWFUL, bitter, oily coffee to get Heather on her feet. Even then she felt exhausted.

A day off, she thought. *My grades are good enough. And one day off doesn't mean I'm falling apart or anything.* She dug in her purse and came up with enough change to cover the coffee, then

Little White Tablet

headed for the door. If anyone asked, she would say that she was sick. That was true enough. And a few hours in bed would be all she needed to get over this. It was probably nothing more than the beginnings of the flu. She went out onto the street and started the walk back to her apartment.

"Heather?"

She looked up, and her mouth dropped open. "Josh?" Her cheeks warmed in embarrassment. *He shouldn't see me like this. I look terrible.*

But Josh didn't seem to notice her appearance. He smiled at Heather and reached out to take her hand. "I didn't expect to run into you this morning."

"Yeah, I was just going to, um, school." Admitting she was going home meant admitting she was sick. And being sick meant no chance to go out.

Josh nodded. "Right. Maybe I should talk to you later. Don't want to stop the education train."

Heather shook her head, then did her best to cover up the pain it caused her. "It's all right," she said. "I've got plenty of time."

"Good. I wanted to ask you about tonight."

"Tonight?" Heather was glad she hadn't said anything about going home. "What are we going to do tonight?"

Josh gave her hand a squeeze. "Something special. Very special. I have something I want to show you."

"What?"

"You'll see tonight," said Josh. He looked at her and frowned. "You feel all right?"

"Sure!" Heather gave the best smile she could manage. "I'm fine."

"You look a little tired."

"Just. . . just didn't get much sleep."

Josh nodded. "I understand. Here, why don't you take one of these?" He dug into his pocket and came up with a small vial. He gave it a quick shake, and a `little white tablet` fell out into his hand.

Heather eyed the pill. All at once, she felt tired in another way. Not tired in her body so much as tired in her head. Josh was offering her drugs. "I. . . uh. . . I don't take drugs."

"That's good because I don't, either." Josh squeezed the little pill in his hand. "These babies are drug-free."

"Then what are they?"

"One hundred percent all natural," Josh insisted. "Scout's honor." He held up two fingers, then three. "Okay, I admit it, I was never a scout. But the tablets are only herbs and vitamins."

Heather took the white pill from his hand and held it between her fingers. "Like a diet pill?"

"Not even that strong."

The coffee hadn't done much to help Heather wake up. Maybe a few herbs were what she needed. She raised the little pill to her mouth and swallowed it down.

MEGAN STOOD WITH HER HANDS ON

Blueprints

her hips and her pointy chin thrust out. "We have just one more chance to get this thing right," she said.

Gaia wondered what it would be like to give her lab partner a nice hard shot to that sharp little chin. Just one. She'd probably run into that pesky little problem of being expelled from school, but it would certainly be satisfying. Maybe then Megan wouldn't be in such a hurry to get in someone's face. "You mean I have one more chance since you and Melanie are just sitting on your asses."

"Well," Megan said with a sniff, "you are the one that messed it up in the first place. It seems only fair that you get to fix it."

Gaia thought about pointing out that she had done all the work in the first place, but she didn't bother. Logic obviously wasn't Megan's best subject. Once again Gaia started through the steps of the experiment. Carefully adding the chemicals, one by one, that would turn the invisible DNA into a measurable mass. She was only about halfway through the experiment when Heather came through the door of the classroom, passed a note to the teacher, and came over to the lab table. Megan and Melanie greeted Heather as if she were the cavalry riding in to save the day.

"Thank God you're here!" said Megan. She gave a sideways glance at Gaia. "She's already ruined the experiment once."

"We have to finish it today or we'll get a zero for the lab," added Melanie.

Heather flashed them both a bright smile. "Don't worry," she said. "I'll help."

Gaia studied Heather. The pants and top she was wearing didn't look like they were part of the Gannis Fall Collection. There was a pinched look to her face, and Gaia thought she could detect the remains of dark circles shining through a double layer of makeup. "Are you okay?" she asked.

"Of course," said Heather. "Why wouldn't I be okay?" She grabbed the lab sheet away from Gaia and scanned the instructions. "How far along are you?"

"About here." Gaia tapped the sheet. "A couple more titrations and then a little cooking and we're done."

"If Gaia doesn't ruin it again," Megan said.

Gaia pressed the tips of her fingers hard against her forehead. What was the caption on that poster in the guidance counselor's office? "Stress is what you feel when you can't choke the living daylights out of the idiot who actually deserves it."

"I messed up," she said. "I think we all understand that I messed up. Now, let's get done so I can get out of here." *Before I'm forced to kill you.* She turned to

Heather again. "So, where were you this morning? And yesterday."

Heather frowned. "I was feeling a little sick before," she said. "Not that it's any of your business. But I'm all better now."

She moved in beside Gaia, and for a few blessed minutes the two worked in silence. As they got down to the bottom of the sheet, Gaia paused again beside the description of DNA. Four compounds. And those compounds could only be mixed in a few ways. Why did that keep sending off little buzzers in her brain?

Gaia was so preoccupied with the note, she barely noticed that Heather and the Heatherettes had started talking. But when something they said caught her attention, she raised her head.

"So," Melanie was saying. "Are you going to see him again this weekend?"

Heather finished stirring the mixture and turned down the heat on the burner. "We're not waiting till this weekend. We're getting together tonight."

"You don't mean with Josh, do you?" asked Gaia.

"Of course with Josh," Heather replied. "Who else would I be seeing?" She grinned at Megan and Melanie. "The next time we're getting together near the school, I'll call you. You need to see this guy. You won't believe how gorgeous he is."

Gaia gritted her teeth. "Didn't I warn you to stay away from Josh?"

"You did, but. . ."

"The guy is a freak."

"Gaia. . ."

"He's dangerous."

"Gaia. . ."

"He's a psycho murderer!" Gaia stopped and realized that she had been talking maybe a little too loud. Maybe a whole lot too loud. Megan and Melanie were looking at her like she was nuts. Nothing too unusual there. Only this time the rest of the room was joining them. The lab seemed momentarily frozen, with everyone staring at Gaia.

Gaia waited until people started to move again, then she lowered her voice and went on. "You need to stay away from Josh if you want to stay alive."

Heather gave her a pitying smile and actually reached out to pat Gaia on the arm. "It's okay. Josh told me."

"Told you what?" asked Gaia.

"About how you broke up. I understand, it must have been very painful."

Gaia shook her head. "What are you talking about? Josh and I were never together."

Heather continued to play the pity pipe. "I know it had to hurt. Especially when he dumped you." Heather glanced toward Megan and Melanie as she made this last sentence. Both girls grew wide, knowing smiles.

The pencil snapped in Gaia's hand. "Josh did *not* dump me."

"Of course not," said Heather. "Because he's not just your everyday psychopathic murderer who just happens to be gorgeous and dress in designer clothes, he's also a compulsive liar with delusions of grandeur." Before Gaia could reply, Heather stuck a glass stirrer into the beaker full of DNA and came out with a pile of shiny, translucent strands. "I think we're done with the experiment."

Megan leaned in closer, her nose prewrinkled in case of smells. "Is that how it's supposed to look?"

Gaia wasn't too sure, either. The mess looked kind of like glass spaghetti, not like the neat double helix that was shown in all the textbooks. Of course, that was just what DNA looked like on a microscopic scale. It was probably stupid to expect any structure like that when dealing with a cup full of the stuff. The transparent strands slipped off the stirrer and fell back into the beaker with a plop.

DNA. Four little compounds in a few simple arrangements. Cytosine, guanine, thymine, and. . .

Gaia froze. The alarms in her head weren't little buzzers now. They were air raid sirens. She snatched the lab sheet back from Heather and confirmed what it said about DNA. Four compounds. Arranged in pairs. Only four combinations.

Now she remembered where she had seen something

like that before. It was on the note, the note she had taken from her father's apartment. The whole bottom half of the note was covered with four colored symbols arranged in pairs. DNA? It had to be. That meant that the note described the DNA of. . . something. But what?

A strange tickling started in the pit of Gaia's stomach. Her uncle had told Gaia that her fearlessness was a result of experiments her father had performed on her as child. That he had given her some drug to drive out fear. Her father said that Gaia being fearless was a fluke. That she was born that way.

What if they were both telling the truth? What if Gaia had been born fearless but born that way because someone had screwed with her DNA, rearranging the compounds to take away the feeling of fear shared by every other human being—every other animal? The note might have the explanation for what had caused the difference.

It could be the blueprints for Gaia Moore.

He had done
it, though.
He had
sliced
open his **russian**
chest and **girl**
handed **roulette**
his
heart to
Gaia on a
silver plate.

"ARE YOU SURE YOU DON'T WANT
something more to eat, Edward?"

Wordless Class

Ed held up the cookie he had been handed. "Uh, no, thanks," he said. "We'll, um, we'll probably get something to eat later, anyway. I need to leave some space."

Natasha smiled at him. "I'm glad that Tatiana met you. She's really enjoyed your company."

"That's great," said Ed. "I mean, she's great." Ed shifted uncomfortably on his chair. He looked at the door hopefully. There was still no sign of rescue. Tatiana's mother seemed perfectly nice. Kind of cool, as parents went, what with the Russian accent and the movie queen looks, but there was only so much time anyone could spend with *anybody's* parents. And Ed had definitely reached his threshold the last time he'd spent quality time with Natasha.

"Have you seen Gaia lately?"

This broad sure knows how to ask the questions. Ed turned his flushed face back to Tatiana's mother. "Not really. She's been keeping a pretty low profile lately."

"That's a shame," said Natasha. "I think Gaia needs good friends. Perhaps even more than my daughter."

Ed wasn't sure how to respond to this. *I agree. And as a matter of fact, I happen to still be in love with Gaia even though I've been spending most of my time going out with your daughter on things that look a lot like dates. So glad you understand.*

For several very long, very uncomfortable seconds they sat and looked at each other. Finally Natasha rose and smoothed down her skirt.

"You must pardon me, but I have to return to my work."

Ed struggled to get to his feet. "I guess I'll clear out. I can come back later."

Natasha held out her hands. "No, no," she said. "The girls will be home anytime now. You're welcome to stay."

This display of hospitality was completely foreign to Ed. He hardly knew how to respond. "Uh. . . okay," was about the most he could come up with as he collapsed back into his chair.

Natasha went to a closet in the corner, took out a long red coat, and shrugged it on. There was an elegance to her movements. A wordless class. There were people from every country in the world all over New York, but something about Natasha made her seem very different from the Russian emigrants that Ed had met in the past. Both Tatiana and Natasha had the same high cheekbones and sculpted features, and a certain. . . attitude. Ed wondered if

Natasha and her daughter were descended from some kind of Russian royalty. The Romanovs of the Upper East Side.

"There is food and drink in the kitchen if you have to wait too long," Natasha said. She gave one last, regal smile and stepped out the door.

Ed relaxed a bit, but not much. He had come here early, knowing that he would beat both Tatiana and Gaia to the house. It was a game. Or a challenge. Russian girl roulette. He didn't really have a name for this game.

It's called being such a totally unbelievable wuss that can't suck it up and get on with life when a girl has dumped you.

A hundred times over the last few days Ed had thought about confronting Gaia. He wanted to find out once and for all what was going on. Why, not an hour after they had made love, she had climbed out of his bed, out of his apartment, and out of his life. Since that day, he had spoken *to* Gaia. Between classes. In the cafeteria. But they hadn't *talked*. And he wanted answers.

He just didn't want the wrong answer.

He didn't want the answer that went, "I woke up and realized that being with you was a really stupid idea. I mean, what the hell was I thinking? Ed Fargo? Me? What a joke. So I got out of there as fast as I could, and I'm never going back."

The possibility of that kind of answer had driven Ed to invent this little game. He would get to the house early. If Tatiana got home first, Ed would take her out to dinner as he had promised. It might look like a date, but Tatiana understood about Ed's Gaia fixation. This would be a nondate date. Nice evening, confrontation-free. If Tatiana and Gaia arrived together. . . Okay, there wasn't much chance of that. Tatiana and Gaia were *never* together. If Gaia got home first, it would be a sign. Maybe not a sign from God, but a sign. Time to Confront Gaia Now.

The front door rattled, and Ed's stomach was suddenly filled with ice. He wondered if he could hide in the coat closet.

Before he could even push himself to his feet, the door opened and Gaia stomped in.

At first she didn't seem to see Ed. She closed the door and started across the room toward the stairs. Gaia looked as gorgeous as Ed had ever seen her. She walked with strong, easy strides, her long legs pressing against the faded gray denim of her jeans. A black sweatshirt was draped over her toned but still curvy form. Her blond hair was held back in a thick, rude, unruly mass that spilled over her shoulders. Her expression was unreadable.

If Tatiana was a Russian princess, Gaia was something else altogether. Gaia was a goddess.

"Hi."

Gaia spun around, one foot moving back, her hands coming up to her sides. Her fingers were locked together, her shoulders slightly turned. Ed recognized the position. Gaia was ready to fight. If she was a goddess, it wasn't the nice "oh, let me help you with those little flowers" kind. Gaia was more the "hey, I think I'll turn your city into gravel" sort of deity.

Her blue eyes locked on Ed like twin lasers. "What are you doing in here?"

"I came—"

"To see Tatiana, right?" Gaia shook her head. "She's not here."

"I know."

"Then why are you here?"

Ed quickly stood up again. He stood with one hand holding the back of his chair, but otherwise he had no support. He thought it was important that he was under his own power when he said these words.

"I love you."

He waited for a moment then, maybe half a heartbeat. Only half because he wanted Gaia to have a chance to shove in an "oh, Ed, I love you, too," but not a whole heartbeat because Ed didn't want Gaia to think he was waiting for those words. Gaia made no reply. This gave Ed an opportunity to cut his losses and run, but he charged on. "I've loved you from the first day you came snarling into my school. I'm not sure I'll ever stop."

Gaia looked at him blankly.

Ed took a deep breath and moved to statement number two. "The night we spent together was the best night of my whole damn life. Best and most important. Not because we had sex. The sex was just sex. I mean, the sex was great. It was the best sex I ever had. Of course, it's not like I had a lot, but. . ." Ed stopped. *Rambling much?* He sucked in another long breath. "What I mean is, you were what made that night important. Being with you. You're beautiful and brilliant and absolutely insane and more scary than anyone I've ever met. There's no one in the world like you."

Ed felt like he had run a marathon. Wearing lead shoes. His breath was coming hard, and his chest was tight. The hand on the back of the chair had gone a bloodless white with the effort of keeping him up.

"I love you," he said again. "I don't know why you left me. I guess I don't give a damn. I just want to be with you." *There. Take that. Who's a wuss?*

For the space of ten very loud heartbeats, Gaia stood at the bottom of the stairs and looked at him. She raised one hand and ran it through the tangle of her hair. She shifted from one foot to the other. Her mouth opened, and Ed thought she was about to reply, but then Gaia's mouth closed again so quickly that her teeth clicked together. Without a single word Gaia turned and started up the stairs.

Halfway up she paused. "Ed?" she said without turning to look at him.

"Yeah?"

"Mind the gap." Gaia sprinted up the rest of the stairs. A second later there was a bang as one of the bedroom doors closed.

Ed choked back disbelieving laughter and dropped into his chair. The gap? What was the damn gap, and what did Gaia mean about minding it? It made no sense.

He had done it, though. He had sliced open his chest and handed his heart to Gaia on a silver plate. He was *not* a wuss. *Just an idiot. A freakin' clown.*

The front door rattled again, and a moment later Tatiana walked in. As soon as she saw Ed, her pretty face brightened. She dropped her books on a table and hurried across the room to give him a kiss on the cheek. "What a nice surprise."

Ed blinked and swallowed. He wondered if he looked bruised. He felt like he had been in some kind of accident. Hit by a bus. Maybe a subway train. He fought back an urge to look down and see if he was leaving blood on the pale, cream-colored carpets.

"You ready to go get something to eat?" His voice

sounded like it came from somewhere else. Another world.

"Of course." She patted a hand against her smooth, flat stomach. "I'm always hungry, and you have promised to show me more sights."

"I'll show you anything you want," Ed said. He forced his face into an expression that he hoped looked something like a smile. He got slowly to his feet, gathered his crutches, and limped toward the door.

Stress might be what you feel when you're not allowed to hurt the person who really deserves it. But try not getting to love the person who deserves it. That's pure agony.

How easy would it be to run back downstairs and grab Ed? Take him back up here with me and and hold him till my arms hurt. Kiss him till my lips go numb. Drag him back to bed and see if the second time really can be better than the first. See if the third time is better than the second. And if the millionth is better than the hundredth.

But none of that is going to happen.

I walked away from Ed because it wasn't safe for me to stay. Not safe for Ed. That hasn't changed. I'm still Gaia, the plague of human misery.

Earthquake Gaia. Hurricane Gaia. Gaiazilla. Stomping on everything I love. Leaving a path of destruction a mile wide no matter where I go.

If I let Ed get too close, he's going to get hurt. Just like Mary. Just like Sam. Just like my mom.

I have to keep him away. I have to make him think I don't care. Because I do.

They say beauty is in the eye of the beholder. I guess that's true enough because I've walked through the Museum of Modern Art and seen all these paintings that are supposed to be priceless. Some of them are cool. More of them look like they were made by throwing snails into a paint pan and letting them crawl away. If beauty's there, count me as a nonbeholder.

I've also seen a lot of reports that say witnesses to a crime are totally unreliable when it comes to remembering details. Guy runs through a building with a beard like Santa Claus, no witness reports a beard. Guy robs a store wearing a blue hat, the witnesses say it was red.

Everything is relative and subjective. I mean, come on, there are people who think Tom Green is funny.

That one night with Gaia was the most important night of my life. Completely earthshaking, life altering, undefeated and untied. The heavyweight champion of nights.

Obviously it wasn't that way for Gaia. She got up from that bed and walked away. And from the way she's acted since then, she had to be absolutely embarrassed by Ed's Big Display of Luv. I definitely didn't feel any warm glow coming back my way.

Oh, Ed, I love you so much, I think I'll just run out of the room mumbling something about a gap. Right. Did she want me to buy new jeans or something?

Gaia doesn't love me. She probably never did. Even if I do still love her, nothing is going to happen. The longer I drag this thing on, the more I'm going to become Ed the Sorry Ass Excuse for a Joke. It's time to get a clue, move along, have a life.

Without Gaia.

THE SMALL MOTOR MADE LITTLE NOISE,

but Tom was careful to turn it off while there were still several hundred yards of surf between the boat

Action Tom

and shore. For a few minutes he let the boat drift. The waves cast pale phosphorescent streaks as they broke above the shallow reef. Farther away, he could see the white lines of foam running up the narrow beach. Beyond that was the chain-link fence of the McHenry Medical College.

It was a bigger place than he had expected. Inside the tall fence a pair of long, two-story buildings peeked up above surrounding palms and mangrove. Smaller buildings were clustered around these two. There were lights at the corners of the buildings and more lights inside. While he watched, Tom saw an elongated shadow move across the space between the buildings and the fence. A moment later another shadow. Guards, he guessed, walking the perimeter.

McHenry College was supposed to be a place mediocre students attended in a last-ditch effort to become doctors. There were many such places scattered over the Caribbean. Students who didn't have the grades to get accepted into a medical school back in the States could slip down here for a couple of years, then hope to find placement in a residency pro-

138

gram back home. Sometimes it worked, more often it didn't, but the students who came to places like McHenry were so desperate to be called doctor, they would take most any risk—and pay most any price.

Up until a few years ago McHenry had been like any other offshore medical school. A hundred or so students had come down each year, a couple dozen had gone north to be doctors. But in 1999 things had changed at McHenry. From that time on, Tom could find no records of students. Not a one. As far as classes were concerned, McHenry Medical College was closed.

Tom looked across the water and watched the lights from the compound reflected in the nighttime sea. Even if there were no classes in anatomy or tests in biochemistry, something was still going on at McHenry. They might not be graduating any doctors, but Tom had a feeling that medical work was being done inside the buildings. Over the years Loki had been involved with genetics, with cloning, with drugs, and with any number of biological horrors. A place like McHenry College would be a perfect cover for more cloning experiments or any other perversions that Loki might think up.

Whatever Loki was doing in the Caymans, Tom was willing to bet the research wasn't going to win any Nobel Prizes. Or help kids in the third world. Or cure the common cold.

The waves pushed the little boat gently over the reef. As soon as it was clear of the breakers, Tom lowered the anchor into the water and let the rope slide silently through his fingers. A moment later the boat surged to a stop seventy feet from the beach. With the boat rising and falling over the low waves, he slipped on his fins and picked up his mask and snorkel. He spit into the mask, then rinsed it with seawater before putting it on. Finally he took his heavy black Glock automatic and slid it into his wet suit before zipping the top closed.

He went over the side of the boat as smoothly as he could, but there was still some splash. Tom waited there, treading water in the dark, to make sure there was no immediate response from the medical compound, then he flipped over on his face and kicked slowly toward shore. He left the snorkel and the flippers on the beach and pulled the gun from his wet suit jacket before heading for the fence.

I am way too old to be playing James Bond, he thought. Of course, so was every actor who ever played James Bond. But those actors had nice stuntmen to take the falls for them, and the bad guys in the movies were never using real bullets. Tom knew that if he kept this up much longer, he was going to catch one of those bullets. Soon.

George Niven had been a field agent once. Tom could remember that George—slim, fast thinking, strong, and decisive. Action George. But time had caught up with Action George and landed him behind a desk. Time was running out for Action Tom as well. It was getting close to the day when Tom would have to find a nice safe desk and a comfortable chair. When he would have to do all his work with his mind and leave the guns and fists to someone else.

He might have already considered such a move if it weren't for Gaia. And Loki. There was no way Tom could sit back and let others take the risks as long as his brother was still out there. Gaia was his responsibility. Loki was his problem. Tom couldn't let either burden slip.

He eased along the fence, looking for an opening. Shadows moved along the inside of the fence, and Tom froze as two men strolled past. They wore white security uniforms, which made good sense for the tropical heat of day but made them stand out like torches in the night. They came closer. Tom crouched down and waited. The men came within a few feet. Tom could have taken them both down before they knew what was going on, but he let them pass. This was a recon mission. If he could get into McHenry, find out what was going on, and get out without being seen, that would be the best-possible outcome. If Loki's operation in this place needed to be stopped. . . that was for another night.

The men moved on, and so did Tom. It took him

five minutes to locate a small gate on the ocean side of the fence. It took ten more for him to open the lock and slip inside without catching the attention of the guards. He hurried across the open grounds and pressed himself to the side of the first building. A quick peek inside a window showed darkened rooms and no people, but he could make out long rows of counters and the glitter of glassware. Laboratories of some kind.

Somewhere nearby a truck rumbled to life. Tom heard distant voices calling and the clatter of an opening gate as the truck pulled away from the compound and rolled out onto the road. He took advantage of the momentary noise and light to hurry around to the door at the front of the building and slip inside. The corridor was empty, dark, and utterly bland. Gray tiled floors. Off-white walls. The only decoration was a biohazard symbol attached to a rank of metal cabinets. There was no one in sight. Tom moved on, his pistol up and ready as he padded down the hallway. At the first door he looked inside and saw more of the lab space. Long black counters. Beakers. Hooded workstations with ranks of petri dishes and Erlenmeyer flasks. There were cardboard boxes on the floor and more boxes stacked on some of the counters. Some of the equipment in the lab was in pieces. It was clear that things at McHenry College were in the process of coming in or going out. Either Loki was still in the middle of scaling up his operations here, or the work was complete.

Tom would have liked to think he had caught this plan early, that whatever plans his brother had for the medical school were just getting started. That Tom had caught this particular bit of evil before it could spread. But McHenry hadn't turned out a student in several years. It was entirely possible, even likely, that Loki had already done what he came for and was finished with this place.

Tom left the silent lab and went to the next door. This time it was an office. Tom poked around inside, searching for any visible papers, but the desk and the file cabinets were completely empty. The next room was another empty office. The next another lab, also full of disassembled equipment and no clues about what had been going on there. That was how it was throughout the whole building. Tom even jogged up the back stairs and looked at the offices on the second floor. Nothing. Even the trash bins and the shredding machines were cleaned out.

A sour taste rose up in Tom's throat. Loki had been working on something here, and it was certainly not a cure for cancer. And it looked as if Tom was too late to stop it.

He went back down the stairs and headed for the back of the building. The final room was a garage and storeroom. A pair of large, dusty trucks stood waiting at the back of the room. Stacked against the wall were more cardboard boxes. The boxes were all identical. Each was about the size of a shoe box, and each was stamped with the words *IKOL—A Global Peace Organization.* Tom nearly laughed at the phrase. *IKOL. LOKI.* And global peace was certainly the opposite of what his brother was after. It seemed too obvious, even for Loki.

The sound of a truck engine came through the open door to the outside, followed by muffled voices. Tom started to go back into the hall but stopped and looked at the boxes. Whatever Loki was shipping out of this place, it would probably be all loaded up and gone by morning. Even if it was too late to stop Loki's plans, Tom could at least get a clue what they were.

There was no time to be subtle. He darted to the nearest box and tore open the top. Inside was a series of smaller boxes. Tom picked up one of these and turned it over in his hands. *Phobosan. 144 Doses,* said the small print at the bottom.

The voices were getting louder. Tom took the small box and retreated into the building. He eased the door shut as quietly as he could and hurried back the way he had come. As he went, he peeled off the top of the box and looked inside. It was hard to tell in the dim light, but he thought the box was full of little tubes. Vials. Each filled with some clear fluid.

What is this? he wondered.

Phobosan Inoculation Schedule: *Subject B*

Phase 1
Initial treatment: GABA enhancers. 180 mg.
Administer orally.

Agent's notes: Dose was delivered by dissolv-
ing tablets in nonalcoholic beverage.

Phase 2
Secondary treatment: Amygdala conditioners.
300 mg. Administer orally.

Agent's notes: Subject took the dosage
directly and willingly.

Phase 3
Tertiary dose: Phobosan. 12 cc. Intramuscular
injection. Must be administered within 48 hours
of phase 2 treatment.

When Heather stopped to think about her life, it was hard *tiny monkeys* to think of a moment when she *wasn't* afraid.

"THIS WAY," SAID JOSH. "ONLY another block to go."

Heather held on to his arm and hurried to keep up. She was starting to feel tired, but not as bad as she had felt before taking Josh's pill that morning. The pill had gone a long way toward kicking the last of the headache and given her an energy boost that lasted all the way into the afternoon. Whatever herbs that thing was made from, Heather was going to have to start buying them by the bottle. "Can't you tell me where we're going?"

The Jumps

Josh shook his head. "I want this to be a surprise. Trust me."

In Heather's experience, a guy that said "trust me" wasn't to be trusted. Guys usually said those words right before they tried to get into your pants. Not that Heather minded in this case. But she didn't think this little expedition they were on was going to lead to a bedroom. Whatever it was that he wanted to show her didn't seem like it would require the removal of clothing.

They walked for blocks. Heather was about to suggest that they grab something to eat before Josh showed her his surprise when he made an abrupt turn and headed for a door at the base of an office building. The door was absolutely bland. Gray metal. No window. No sign. Not even a buzzer. Josh led Heather up to the door and stopped.

"This is the place," he said.

"Here?" Heather tipped back her head and looked up at the building. It wasn't very impressive. Just one of those drab places that filled in the spots between more interesting buildings. Not too tall. Not too new. Just there. "How do we get in?"

"That won't be a problem," said Josh. No sooner had he stopped speaking than there was a click from the door. Josh grabbed the handle and pulled it open. He stepped to the side and swept his arm toward the door. "After you."

Heather felt a little chill down in her stomach. The building was absolutely ordinary, and she did trust Josh. Really, she did. But there was something about this place that gave her a major case of the jumps. She swallowed hard and stepped through the door.

Inside, the building seemed much newer and larger than she had expected. The hallway was very wide, very bright, and very, very long. The floor and walls were both clean and almost spotless white. There were a few abstract paintings hung along the walls to give a hint of color. The lights were. . . Heather couldn't see any lights anywhere. There just *was* light, as if the walls and floor and ceiling were all putting off their own illumination. The corridor stretched out ahead, white and empty and apparently endless.

"This place is bigger on the inside than it is on the outside," said Heather.

Josh stepped past her with a laugh. "That's just an illusion, but it is way large. Come on. You haven't seen anything yet."

They walked on down the hallway. Heather's heels clicked against the tiled floor. After what seemed to Heather like at least another two blocks of walking, they came at last to a series of ordinary wooden doors. Josh didn't hesitate—he walked up to one of the doors and pushed it open. This time Heather followed him into a room that was large, but not huge. It was obviously a lab of some sort. Several people dressed in white coats were working at computers. There were benches covered in gleaming glassware and instruments with the soft sheen of brushed stainless steel.

That Josh would bring her to a lab was strange enough. Stranger was that the lab was also full of animals. In Plexiglas cages Heather could see dogs of all sizes, cats of all colors, and even some tiny monkeys with fierce, angry expressions on their small, white-furred faces.

Heather spun slowly around. "What is this place?"

"This is where I work," said Josh.

"Work? I thought you went to school."

"I do. Sometimes." Josh held up one hand and waved to a man across the room. "Dr. Glenn!" he called. "This is the girl I was telling you about."

Heather looked at Josh and scowled. "Why were you telling someone about me?" she asked in a low voice. "What were you telling him?"

"All good things, naturally," said Josh.

An older man in an open white coat approached from across the room. He had a short salt-and-pepper beard, a round, friendly face, and pale blue eyes behind thick wire-frame glasses. "Hello," he said. "I'm glad you agreed to come in to see us."

The man held out his hand. Heather let go of Josh's arm long enough to shake the man's hand. Despite his broad smile, Heather still felt afraid. "I don't even know where herc is."

The man with the beard seemed startled. "Josh, didn't you tell your friend about us?"

Josh gave a little wince. "Actually, I wanted her to be surprised."

"Hmmph." The man shook his head. "I'll bet she *is* surprised, but I wouldn't doubt that she's also a bit frightened." He turned back to Heather, his smile wider than ever. "I'm Dr. Edward Glenn."

"Heather Gannis, nice to meet you," Heather said automatically. "Is someone going to tell me where I am?"

"This place is called IKOL," the doctor replied. "We do medical work on a private grant."

"Oh," said Heather. The answer was a little comforting but still confusing. Why would Josh want to bring her to this place? "What kind of medical work do you do?"

Josh stepped around Dr. Glenn. "Only the coolest kind," he said. "Come and see."

Heather followed the two men to the other side of the lab. In between a pair of glowing computer screens was a set of small, transparent boxes. The left box held a little cat, hardly more than a kitten. The right box held two tiny white mice. The center box was empty except for a screen of white material that ran down the center.

"Prepare to be amazed," said Josh. "Step one, the predator." He popped open the first box and took out the cat. He gave its fur a quick stroke, then lowered it into the box. "And now the prey." This time Josh went for the mice. It took him a few tries, but after a moment he had both of the white mice in his hands. He dropped them into the center box with the cat but on the other side of the screen.

Josh turned around and raised his eyebrows. "Okay," he said. "Here comes a miracle." He put a hand to the screen.

"Wait!" Heather grabbed for his arm. "If you take that out, the cat will eat them."

152

"There's a glass plate," said Josh. He put his knuckles inside the box and rapped on the invisible barrier. "The mice are safe."

Quickly he moved his hand back to the screen and whipped it upward. The cat spotted the mice instantly. It jumped forward, its claws slashing against the glass and a low rumble pouring from its throat.

On the other side of the barrier the mice had seen the cat as well. One of the mice ran for the far end of the box. It scrambled to get up the wall, slipped, tried again, then ran madly around the box, looking for an escape. The other mouse didn't move.

"Well," said Josh. "What do you think?"

Heather shrugged. "I don't know," she said. "What am I supposed to think?"

Josh reached into the box and snatched up the mouse that was running madly. He held the little rodent out toward Heather. "See how fast this guy is breathing? He's terrified."

Heather didn't appreciate having the animal so close to her face, but she nodded. "Of course he's scared. The cat's about to eat the poor thing."

"The cat's not going to eat him," said Josh. "The glass keeps him safe. The mouse is just *afraid* the cat will get him."

"So?"

"So look at the other mouse." Josh plopped the

panicked mouse back into its original box and pointed at the second mouse.

The second mouse seemed absolutely calm. It sat only an inch from the glass where the cat clawed and scratched, but it made no move to run.

Heather leaned over the glass and looked at it. The mouse certainly appeared to see the cat; it just didn't seem to care. "What's wrong with it?" she asked.

"Nothing's wrong with it," said Josh. "Something's *right* with it."

"Did you tranquilize it?"

Josh shook his head. "It's fully awake. Fully aware. It's just not afraid."

Heather thought for a moment. "How can it not be afraid?"

Dr. Glenn stepped forward. "That's the break-through we've been working on. We've isolated a neurotransmitter called GABA. It's a chemical in the brain that acts to regulate anxiety. We've learned how to modify the operation of this transmitter." He tapped the glass beside the mouse. "This little fel-low is the culmination of years of work. Absolutely fearless."

"Fearless," Heather repeated. She looked at the mouse. So tiny, but unafraid. "If it's fearless, won't it just walk off the table or something like that and get hurt?"

"It's not insensible," said Dr. Glenn. "Its reasoning

is completely unimpaired. In fact, you might say that this animal is thinking more clearly than it ever has before. Its thinking is unclouded by unreasonable fears and nervousness."

Josh put a hand on the doctor's shoulder. "You think I could talk to Heather alone for a few minutes? I'd like to explain to her what comes next."

Dr. Glenn nodded. "Of course, of course." He straightened up and looked at Heather. "Very nice to meet you, Ms. Gannis. I hope we'll be seeing you again soon."

Heather stared at the man's back as Dr. Glenn walked away, then she spun around to face Josh. "What's going on here? Why did you tell him about me? What do you mean, 'what comes next'? Why are you showing me these things?"

"It's a little hard to explain." Josh leaned against the counter and reached down to stroke the trapped cat. "You remember me telling you that I knew Gaia?"

"Gaia?" Heather clenched her teeth. *Does every conversation have to be about Gaia?* "Did you bring her here first?"

"Not exactly." Josh gave the cat another stroke, and it leaned against his hand. "Look, you like Gaia, don't you?"

"Like her!" Heather rolled her eyes. "Why would I like Gaia? She's ruined everything since she got here."

"But you like her, anyway. And you hate her. That's

the thing, see—no matter how irritating Gaia is, she's still fascinating. Right?"

"I don't—"

"Come on. Tell the truth."

Heather shook her head rapidly, sending her dark hair flying. "I don't like her. Not exactly."

"Maybe it's more like you're jealous of her," suggested Josh.

Heather glared at him and stood up straighter. There had been very few turns on the way to this place. She was sure that she could find her way back home without Josh, and she was ten seconds away from leaving. She didn't like the way this conversation was going *at all*. "You think I should be jealous of Gaia?"

"No."

"You think she's smarter than I am?"

"No."

"Prettier?"

"Absolutely not." Josh stopped stroking the cat and folded his arms across his chest. "But there's one thing that Gaia has that you don't. It's the one thing that makes her so attractive. It's the reason that Gaia is always at the center of things."

Heather narrowed her eyes. "She's certainly become the center of this conversation." She paused for a moment, then she nodded. "All right. What is it? What makes Gaia so special?"

"She's fearless."

It took a few seconds for the words to process through Heather's mind. When they did, her eyes went wide. Thinking back, it made sense. "You mean, like the mouse. . . Did she take something?"

Josh picked up a folder from the table and opened it. Inside was a picture of a young girl. Blue-eyed, with blond hair chopped off at chin length. Despite the rounded, baby-fat face Heather had no trouble telling that this was a picture of a very young Gaia Moore. "When Gaia was only a couple of years old," said Josh, "her father injected her with a prototype of the fearless serum. It was dangerous; I can't even tell you how dangerous. The serum hadn't been perfected or tested. It could have done anything. It could have left Gaia permanently damaged. It might have killed her."

Heather took the picture from Josh's hand and looked down at the chubby cheeks of little Gaia Moore. "But it worked."

"That's right," said Josh. "It worked. Ever since that day Gaia has been completely, totally without fear."

A thousand moments went through Heather's mind. She could remember a lot of times when Gaia seemed angry. A few times when she seemed nice. But she couldn't think of one time when Gaia had been really worried or afraid. Could it be true? "Fearless." The word felt strange in her mouth.

"Think of it." Josh took both of Heather's hands in his own. "Never having to be afraid." The idea was almost too fantastic to believe. When Heather stopped to think about her life, it was hard to think of a moment when she wasn't afraid. Afraid she wouldn't fit in or wouldn't get a good grade. Afraid she wouldn't get into a good college. Afraid she would.

Afraid that Gaia Moore would steal any guy Heather so much as looked at twice.

People thought Heather was perfect, that she had everything, but they didn't realize how hard she worked to create and maintain that façade.

She looked up at Josh. "I still don't understand why you brought me here."

"I brought you here because I like you." He squeezed her hands. "And because I wanted to give you a gift."

"Gift?"

Josh nodded. "It was dangerous when Gaia's father gave her the serum, but that's not true anymore. A lot of people have been working on this thing for more than a decade. It's been tested in every way you can imagine. It's completely safe."

"Safe for people?"

"Yeah. Safe for people."

"Like me?"

"That's why you're here." Josh leaned in close, and

his voice dropped to a whisper. "Let me give you the same advantage that Gaia has over everyone else. Let me make you free. Let me make you fearless."

GAIA SAT ON A LOW STONE BENCH

Unseen People

half a block from the United Nations building and clenched her jaw against the cold. There were still lights in a handful of the monolith's offices. Gaia wondered if Natasha was in one of them, still translating speeches or documents for the Russian government. Gaia didn't have a watch on, but she knew it was getting late. She yawned. This was worse than marching around on `mugger patrol`. At least on patrol Gaia stayed warm and there was some chance of a little entertainment. The only thing she was getting by sitting around on this bench was a frozen butt.

She was beginning to wonder if she had misunderstood the directions when a gray Mercedes sedan pulled over to the curb. The power window slid down smoothly.

"Hurry," George Niven said from inside the car. "Get in."

Gaia scrambled off the bench and into the car. The

sedan was rolling even before she got her door shut. They moved out into traffic, made a quick left-hand turn, and headed toward Midtown at axle-breaking speed.

George glanced at the rearview mirror. "I don't think we're being followed, but I can't be sure."

"Followed?" Gaia twisted around and looked out the back window. She saw a lot of headlights back there. Exactly how did you figure out which ones were after you? "You think some of Loki's people were following you when you picked me up?"

"No." George shook his head. "I'm fairly certain that they don't care about me. It's you they were after."

"Me?" Gaia stared at the headlights. "I was all alone back there. No one was around."

"These people are professionals, Gaia. You wouldn't see them if they didn't want to be seen."

The whole idea that she was being followed by these unseen people was way weird. "How did they find me? I came straight here when I found your note. I didn't tell anyone where I was going."

George glanced over at her. "They know where you're staying. They've been following you frequently. Most of the time, in fact."

"For how long?"

"Weeks. Months. Maybe longer." George turned his attention back to the road as he turned onto Broadway.

"The information I've collected shows that you've rarely been out of their sight."

Gaia might not be able to feel fear, but this information made her feel like she had swallowed a bowling ball. They had been watching her. Had they seen her fights in the park? Where had they been, standing back in the trees? When she had fallen unconscious from exhaustion, had they timed how long she lay on the ground? If what George said was true, then these people knew her every weakness. They knew what she was capable of, and they knew all the people who mattered to her. She had been right to stay away from Ed. If these people were watching, then there was no doubt they had already seen Gaia and Ed together. If she could convince them that she didn't care about Ed anymore, then Ed would be safe.

George might not have the evidence, but she was ready to convict. If these people had been watching her all that time, then every terrible thing that had happened was their fault. They had a lot of blood on their hands. "Do you think this is all part of Loki's organization?" she asked finally, breaking the silence.

George nodded without turning away from the window. "I can't establish that for sure, but it's likely."

Gaia considered this for a moment, then went on. "I think I have an idea."

161

"What?"

"A few days ago I sent my uncle an e-mail."

George turned around quickly. "You did what?"

"I sent him an e-mail. I wanted to know where my father was."

George had a disturbed look on his face. "Gaia, you have to be more careful in the future. If your uncle is involved with these activities against your father, you could be putting yourself into terrible danger by making contact."

"What danger?" said Gaia. "If those bozos are watching me every minute, I'm already in about as much danger as I can get. Anyway, the e-mail was part of the plan."

George looked like he was about to issue another warning, but he stopped. "What plan??" he asked. "What is this idea of yours?"

"I want to arrange a meeting with my uncle. Drag him out in the open and trap him."

"Trap him how?" asked George.

"I don't know that part yet." Gaia pushed her hair back from her face and looked out at the people passing by on the sidewalk. "He must be wanted for something. . . ."

"Yes. . . ," George said slowly. "I think you could say that the intelligence community would like to have a very long discussion with Mr. Loki."

Gaia nodded. "Then that's it. I arrange for a meeting

with my uncle. You arrange to have the CIA standing by." With that, Gaia put her hand on the door handle and started to get out of the car.

George leaned across the seat and grabbed her left arm. "Wait!" he said. "There's something else I need to talk to you about."

Gaia eased back into her seat. "What?"

"Remember when I told you that someone your father trusts is passing his information on to Loki?"

"That doesn't worry me," Gaia said. "My father doesn't trust anybody."

George pressed his lips into a thin line. "He trusts Natasha enough to watch his only daughter."

Gaia stared at him. "You think Natasha is a spy for Loki?"

"We're not sure," George said with a shrug. "However, she seems to be the most likely candidate." His expression softened. "Gaia, come back with me. I'll keep you safe until we can think of the next move."

"No." Gaia put her hand to the door again, and this time she climbed out before George could make any move to stop her. She leaned back through the door. "You get ready to take down Loki. I have to keep an eye on Natasha. If she really is a spy, I'll find out." She closed the door of the sedan and walked quickly away.

JOSH TAPPED THE GLASS AND SCOWLED

at the unmoving mouse. "This thing's really okay?"

A Thin Smile

"So far, all indications are that the treated mouse is fine," replied Dr. Glenn. "It's only fearless. That much was completely true."

Josh worked to make sure his voice stayed level. Uninterested. "And it will be the same with the girl, right? She'll be fearless but unharmed."

"That's what we're hoping for. Why? Are you concerned for this Heather person?"

"I. . ." Josh shook his head. "Of course not. I'm just curious." He tapped the glass again. "And bored. Does His Bossiness always have to be late?"

Dr. Glenn stood behind him with his hands shoved down into the pockets of his white lab coat and his glasses pushed back on his forehead. "I'm sure that he would tell you that he's never late. Whenever he arrives is the correct time."

Josh snorted. "Yeah, I'm sure he would." He gave the glass tank another loud flick with his finger. "That's because he doesn't have to wait around all damn night for someone to show up."

"Feel free to complain when he gets here," said Dr. Glenn. "You won't mind if I stand over here and watch? It should be interesting."

"No, thanks. I'm kind of fond of breathing."

A door opened at the far end of the room. Josh straightened and turned to face the door as a tall man with short-cropped hair and broad shoulders under a khaki trench coat strolled into the room. "Good evening, sir."

Loki advanced across the room in four long strides. "I understand that our new subject paid a visit tonight." He shrugged out of his coat and let it fall. Dr. Glenn darted forward and grabbed the coat before it could touch the ground.

"She was here," said Josh. "We've showed her the effects and given her the preliminary information. Just as you ordered, sir."

"That's good. Excellent. And did she immediately agree to participate?"

Josh hesitated. "Uh, no."

Loki looked at him and raised one eyebrow. "No?"

"Heather. . . the subject. . . she wanted some time to think about it. You told me not to press her. To let her think it was her own decision."

"I did. However, I'd hoped you would be a more effective salesman." The big man strolled around the room with his hands clasped behind his back. "How would you read her mood? Do you think she's in?"

Josh nodded quickly. "Yes. Absolutely. She's so jealous of the first subject that she'll never be able to resist our offer. By tomorrow she'll be begging to participate." He gave a nervous smile. "And she's taken the two oral treatments. That's making her a lot more open to suggestion as well as lowering her normal barriers."

Loki looked at him for several seconds. Josh had a hard time standing still under the steady gaze of Loki's pale blue eyes. "Then why didn't she agree tonight?"

"Tomorrow," said Josh. "I'm positive."

"Good," Loki said. "I like people who are positive." He put a hand on Josh's shoulder and applied a pressure that was just one stop away from painful. "Tomorrow will be fine. So long as we have the second subject in the program within forty-eight hours, everything will be fine."

Dr. Glenn cleared his throat. "We can inject the girl at any time. The phobosan can be even delivered by dart if need be."

"No," Loki said sharply. "The subject has to think it's her own idea. That's critical." Loki released his grip on Josh's shoulder and returned to his restless pacing around the room. "She has to think that she already contained the seeds of fearlessness before she took the treatment."

Josh shook his head. "I don't understand why it's so important what everybody thinks."

"Hearts and minds," said Loki. "Hearts and minds." He tapped a finger against the side of his head. "If you really want to control people, you have to control how they *think*. We convince Heather that we can make her fearless through drugs. We plant information that convinces Gaia that she is fearless because of genetics.

It doesn't matter what they believe as long as they stay away from the truth."

"And what is the truth?" asked Josh.

Loki stopped in front of the tank where the cat and the mouse still waited on opposite sides of the glass plane. "The truth isn't important. What's important is keeping Gaia and your little friend in doubt. Doubt is the enemy of power."

Loki's even white teeth showed through in a thin smile. "Trust me." He pointed at the mouse and turned his head to look at Josh. "This is one of ours?"

Josh nodded. "Full treatment," he said. "That's the one we used in our demonstration to the new subject."

"Oh, really?" Loki looked at the mouse for a moment longer, then he grabbed the top of the glass barrier and pulled it from the cage.

The mouse didn't react. It stood where it had been all evening, its fine whiskers twitching in the air. Fearless. The cat stood for only a second, then it crouched down and leaped. There was a short squeal and a crunch as the mouse was caught in the cat's sharp incisors.

Loki laughed. "Perfect," he said. "Perfect." He let the glass barrier clatter on the countertop and spun to face Josh once again. "Never forget: fear is and always has been a survival instinct."

Everything had changed, only not really. The goals were still the **loaded** **revolver** **a** same: Stop Loki, get a life.

GAIA SLID HER KEY INTO THE LOCK

as softly as possible, eased open the door, and slipped into the apartment. She'd already come to terms with the fact that her little escape fantasy would have to be postponed. In the meantime she had some information to gather.

Kremlin Security

The entranceway was dark and quiet. A soft gleam of light came from the kitchen, and a table lamp lent a pool of light to the top of the stairs. All the other rooms, including the bedrooms, were dark.

She did a quick, quiet circuit through the rooms on the first floor. No annoying Tatiana in the living room. No `traitor Natasha` in the kitchen. Only nice, empty, quiet rooms.

Upstairs was more of the same. Gaia poked her head into each bedroom and bathroom. No one. She leaned against the wall at the top of the stairs. *If this place was like this all the time, I might actually like it here.*

An overly ornate clock on the wall began a series of soft musical chimes. Eleven. How could it only be eleven? Considering everything that had happened, she thought eleven seemed awfully early. Still, what were Tatiana and Natasha doing out so late? Natasha was probably still working. Or if George was right, maybe she was out meeting with Loki. There was little doubt about what Tatiana was doing. Tatiana was out with Ed.

Most of the blame for the Ed and Tatiana connection was solidly in the bony lap of a little Russian girl. All those big-eyed looks and the bumbled English. Little touches on the arm. Laughing at jokes that were way short of funny. Gaia had never seen anyone deliver such a full-court flirt. But that didn't mean Ed got off with zero blame. How could he mean the things he had said to Gaia, then turn around and spend his nights with Tatiana? True, Gaia had pushed him away, but that didn't make it right. He should have waited.

Waited for hell to freeze over or Gaia Moore's life to make sense, whichever came first.

Gaia pushed herself away from the wall. All right, the Russian royalty was out making time with the serfs. How best to take advantage of this breach in Kremlin security?

The first target was Natasha's closet. She found a collection of business clothes, a couple of formal gowns, and a surprising number of shoes—weren't they supposed to be short on stuff in Russia? But there was nothing that would tie Natasha to Loki.

Next Gaia went through the dresser. The first two drawers there held no surprises. The third held a gun.

Gaia lifted the weapon and studied it in the light.

Revolver. Thirty-eight caliber. The pistol was small but heavier than she would have thought. Gaia's father had taught her to handle weapons when she was eight. She wielded a gun capably. It had been a while, but Gaia was sure that she could still put five rounds in a three-inch pattern, or reload a spent shell, or fieldstrip an M-16 if the situation came up. That didn't mean she liked guns.

Gaia fingered the release and flipped open the side of the revolver. It was loaded. Five shells and an empty chamber under the hammer. That was a sensible precaution to cut down on accidents. Not that keeping a loaded revolver in your dresser could be described as anything like sensible.

There were some additional bullets in a small cardboard box in the same drawer where Gaia had found the gun—another good sign that Natasha hadn't been thinking of safety when she'd stashed the gun here. She'd wanted access to a weapon, and she'd wanted it quickly. Both the gun and the ammo were American made. Neither of them proved that Natasha was working with Loki. But they were definitely suspicious. As far as Gaia knew, a loaded revolver wasn't exactly standard equipment for a UN translator.

She flipped the gun closed and put it carefully back into its nest of lace underwear and woolen socks. There was nothing so interesting in the next drawer or in the bottom drawer. Gaia went on to the table beside the bed. She found a couple of fat novels waiting there in the table drawer. One English. One Russian. You couldn't fault Natasha for staying in practice.

Gaia put the novels back into the drawer and started to close it, but it was reluctant to shut. She pulled open the drawer, rearranged the books, and tried again. Still no luck. Something was blocking the drawer. Gaia flattened out her hand and stuck her fingers far back into the drawer, reaching around the edges. Something was back there, all right, but she could only brush it with her fingertips. She knelt down and looked inside. Metal. A metal box.

Another thirty seconds of fiddling with the drawer got Gaia no closer to reaching the box. So she changed her approach. One sharp pull popped the drawer from its mounting and left it dangling in Gaia's hands. Novels, paper clips, and a worn nail file went thumping to the floor. Gaia tossed the drawer onto the bed and reached her hand into the opening. This time the metal box came out easily. It was small, no more than an inch thick and maybe eight inches long. Gaia opened the hinged lid and looked inside.

Bingo.

Envelopes. The box was full of envelopes. Gaia gave them a quick flip through with her thumb. There had to be a dozen of them here, and something was inside each of them. From the way they were hidden, Gaia could guess that she had found Natasha's secret orders.

Gaia opened the first envelope and pulled out the page inside.

Natasha,

I want to thank you again for the time you spent showing me around your city. Though I had visited Moscow many times in the past, I cannot remember any visit nearly so pleasant.

I'd also like to thank you for sharing your memories of Katia. I never knew her as a child, and even as adults our time together seemed far too short. Listening to your stories opened up decades that I knew very little about.

I hope that in time we'll be able to meet again and I'll learn more about Katia's family. These will be wonderful stories to pass on to my daughter.

Sincerely,
Tom Moore

Gaia read through the note again. Not from Loki at all, but from her father. She wondered what kind of stories Natasha had told about her mother. Natasha had never told any of these stories to Gaia. Neither had her father.

There was no date on the note, but it had obviously been written several months ago. Maybe even years. At the time, Natasha had still been living in Russia, and there was no mention of meeting her in New York. It irritated Gaia to see her father being so friendly with Natasha, but it seemed like a pretty ordinary letter.

So why did Natasha save it, and why did she hide it in her little stash?

Maybe she had saved it because she was spying for Loki, but even if that were true, there didn't seem to be much in the letter worth saving. No secret information there.

The next letter in the stack had a smudged postmark from Istanbul and was written on stationery from the Grand Atatürk Hotel. Gaia unfolded the single sheet and put it down on top of the first letter.

Dear Natasha,

> *Your letter eventually reached me, though not as quickly as I would have liked.*

> *It's been a long time since we were together. Too long. Hopefully, if everything works out, that will soon change.*

> *I think your suggestion on how to handle the*

175

situation with Gaia is a good one. In fact, I'm thrilled at the idea. You have no idea how much time I have spent worrying about this situation. Or perhaps you do, since you have a daughter of your own.

In any case, having Gaia close to someone I trust will be a great comfort. As soon as I return from this engagement, we'll get together and work out the details.

Looking forward to seeing you again,

Tom

This second letter was a bit more disturbing to Gaia. In the first place it seemed a lot more, well, *friendly*.

It had clearly been written after the first. How long after, Gaia couldn't tell. Natasha might have still been in Moscow when the letter was written, but it was clear she was already in a New York state of mind. Of course, no one had ever consulted Gaia on where she wanted to live and whom she wanted to live with. Why should they bother with that? And she was sure that her father never thought for a second about Gaia moving in with him. No way. Completely inconvenient. That was out of the question.

She grabbed the next letter out of the stack. Plain old business envelope this time, with no return address.

Inside was another single-sheet letter. Tom was nothing if not brief.

> *Dear Natasha,*
> *This is a very difficult letter for me to write. Not because I have bad news, but because I've become so unfamiliar with good news, I don't know how to react to it. The time we spent in New York was wonderful. And I think the only possible reason for this is that you are wonderful. When I'm with you, all the things that have so weighed down the last few years seem to float away.*

Gaia stopped reading at that point and closed her eyes. There was a tightness in her throat and a bitter, sour taste at the back of her mouth. When had this letter been written? Had Gaia still been at George and Ella's? Maybe even when she'd been laid up in the hospital. Whenever it had been written, it was clear that her father—her father who never had time to talk to her—had plenty of time to talk to Natasha. While Gaia was going through one horror after another, her father had time to run around New York with his gun-toting girlfriend. Had they gone shopping together? They'd probably taken in a Broadway show and had a nice dinner at some place where the waiter handed over the wine cork.

Not only had her father ignored Gaia, it seemed like he had completely forgotten about her mother.

In my dreams, we are never separated. We can live together somewhere where it's peaceful, where it's safe, where neither of us has to face the difficulties we now live with every day.

The paper started to crunch in Gaia's hand. Difficulties that they faced every day. Yeah, her father went traipsing around the world with his girlfriend and then whined because they couldn't shack up together. Natasha had this great place in New York and probably a palace back in Russia. In the meantime Gaia had nothing. *Oh, yeah, I feel so sorry for you two.*

Most of all, I dream of a place where Gaia and Tatiana can worry about their grades and their boyfriends and what they're going to wear to the prom. I want to deal with helping them through tough calculus exams and picking out universities and teach the girls to drive. I want to throw a party for my daughter's eighteenth birthday, not worry about whether she'll live to see nineteen. I want to see her walk down the aisle at her high school graduation, at her college graduation, at her wedding.

More than anything, I want to tell her about

her mother, about me, and about why we made the choices we did. I want to tell her just how proud she has made me every day.

And because I want these things, I know that I can't be close to her. Or to you. Every time I talk to Gaia, every time I'm close to her, only increases the risk. Until this situation is finally and completely resolved, all the things I want— we want—will remain no more than dreams.

A drop of water hit the letter. Gaia wiped it away with her thumb and tried to read the next sentence, but another drop followed the first. It wasn't until the ink was blurred by a third drop that Gaia realized the water was coming from her eyes. She put the letter down and rubbed at her face.

He cares. He remembers me.

Gaia's throat went tight, and she squeezed her eyes shut. How long had it been since she'd dared to think that her father cared about her? How long had it been since she'd thought he might actually love her?

She opened her eyes, rubbed away the latest tears, and started to read the next part of the letter. Suddenly that didn't seem like such a good idea. Reading letters that were about spying was one thing. Reading her father's love letters to Natasha. . . That was just wrong in so many ways.

Working as quickly as she could, Gaia shoved the letters back in their envelopes and put them all back in the box. Then the box went back into the table, the crap from the floor went back in the drawer, and the drawer slid in over the box. With careful placement Gaia even managed to put the two novels back inside the drawer before she closed it. Finally she turned off the lights and stepped out of Natasha's bedroom.

Gaia stood at the top of the hallway and tried to think of her next step. Her head was swimming. She felt a faint shadow of that weird feeling from the fear serum tingling down in her guts. Everything had changed, only not really. The goals were still the same: Stop Loki, get a life. Except now, more than any time since her mother's death, the idea of a life that was, okay, maybe not normal, but *close*, seemed just out of reach.

Her planning was interrupted when the door opened and Tatiana came in, grinning from ear to ear. A grin that was no doubt Ed induced.

Tatiana started to take off her coat. When Gaia entered her field of vision, that smile turned instantly into a frown. "What are you doing?"

"Thinking," said Gaia.

"Humph." Tatiana finished taking off her coat and put it into the closet. "Thinking. . . I never saw you do that. Yelling, yes. Fighting—sometimes. But not thinking."

So much for our little truce, Gaia thought. Whatever post–butt-kicking afterglow Tatianna had been basking in the other night after their fight with Gen and her drug dealer boyfriend had now faded.

Gaia put her hands on the railing at the top of the stairs and squeezed. One thing was sure: If she could get rid of Loki and have something that looked like a normal life, that life was going to have Ed in it. It didn't matter what was going on between Ed and Tatiana. Gaia was going to have him back. She stomped down the stairs and headed for the front door.

"Where are you going?" asked Tatiana.

"Out."

"It's nearly midnight. You shouldn't go out now."

"You were out," said Gaia. "Natasha is still out."

"My mother's at work." Tatiana reached out, as if she were going to take Gaia's arm, then she changed her mind and let her hands drop to her sides. "What are you doing?"

"I've got work. I've got very important work to do." Gaia stepped outside and slammed the door behind her.

How many times have I wished for it? A normal life. Sounds like a pretty sucky wish, doesn't it? I mean, why not wish for a million dollars? But what I really want is time with my father, a chance to be with Ed without worrying about getting him killed, a chance to breathe.

I've always had this problem trying to understand why my father stayed away from me. Now I know. Ed.

I don't mean my father stays away from me because of Ed. No, but the thing with Ed and me is a great example. The reason I stay away from Ed is because I'm afraid to let the slimeballs who are watching me know that I care about him. I've even let Ed think I didn't like him. Let him hate me, maybe. But only because I have to. Only to keep him safe.

And that's the way it is for my dad. He stays away from me

because that's what he thinks it will take to keep me away from Loki. I think he's wrong. If he would only come to me, we'd be stronger. We could plan together. Work together.

I don't know. Maybe Ed thinks the same thing about me.

It doesn't matter now. The only thing that's important is to end all this. Stop Loki. Stop all the killing. Rescue not just my dreams, but also my father's. He can be with Natasha—I wouldn't mind first finding out what the loaded gun is for, but he can be with her. He can be with me. Maybe we'll all get a nice little house and a golden retriever and a white picket fence.

Okay, so I don't even want that stuff. But we can get what we do want. Act the way we want with the people we want without worrying about psycho gunmen and cloned killers.

If my father marries Natasha, this new life will mean having

Tatiana for a sister, and I can
live with that. I think.

   But if sis thinks she's going
to get Ed without a fight, she's
got a big surprise coming.

GEORGE STRUGGLED TO TIE THE BELT

Sleepless

on his robe as he made his way down the stairs. The pounding at the door came again.

"Hold on," he said. "I'm coming."

He removed the first chain on the door, then stopped to look through the peephole. What he saw made him scramble to open the other locks. He flung open the door and stared out on the small porch. "Gaia," he said. "My God. What are you doing here?"

Gaia Moore smiled at him from a face that was nearly hidden behind a tangle of thick blond hair. Her blue eyes were so bright, they seemed to glow. "I had to talk to you. I wanted to see if you had worked out how we could trap Loki."

George looked around quickly, then he took Gaia's arm and pulled her into the brownstone. "You shouldn't have come here. You have to get out of sight."

As soon as Gaia was through the door, George slammed it shut and looked again through the peephole. The early morning street appeared empty, but George wasn't fooled. They were out there somewhere. Watching. He turned his attention back to Gaia.

The girl was rarely what George would have

considered well-groomed, but usually she was at least passable. Now she looked as though she had been sleeping under the platform at Grand Central. Then he had another thought. "Have you slept at all?"

Gaia shook her head. She shrugged back the curtain of blond waves. "I was busy working on some ideas."

She looked thinner than she had when she'd lived in the brownstone. The fine angles and high cheekbones of her face seemed more exposed. She seemed more vulnerable. Fragile. George knew well enough that much of that appearance was an illusion. This girl possessed strength and abilities that were beyond those of most full-grown men. Still, it was obvious that Gaia needed rest.

"Look," he said. "Your old bedroom is still just as you left it. Why don't you go upstairs and sleep for a few hours? Then we can talk."

Gaia shook her head. "We have to catch Loki."

"Of course," said George. "And we will." He took his hand away from her arm and gave what he hoped was a comforting smile. "Actually, maybe it's a good thing you came. I have more information, and I think it would be a good idea if you stayed here from now on."

"Can't." Gaia paced around in a restless circle. "Look, I just came over to. . . to. . . I don't know. But things are different." She took a deep breath. "We have to stop Loki now so my dad can get together with Natasha."

"Natasha?"

Gaia nodded, still walking around and around the living room. "I know you don't like her, but I found out that my father and Natasha are in love. My dad can still have a life. I can still have a life. We just have to stop Loki so they can get together."

George leaned against the back of a padded armchair. Suddenly he felt very old and very tired. "Gaia. That's not going to happen."

"Why not?" she demanded.

"It's much more complicated than that."

Gaia stopped and turned to him. There was a painful mixture of hope and exhaustion on her face. *How long has it been since she really rested?* George wondered. *Not just slept, but rested.* Gaia was only seventeen, but there was a century of exhaustion on her young face. "Gaia, I have information that links Natasha to Loki."

"That's what you said before, but it can't be right because—"

"It is. I was contacted this evening. Natasha and Loki were seen together last night. They may still be together."

"That's a lie," she wailed.

"I'm afraid it's not," George said with a sigh. Natasha

is probably with Loki right now, plotting against your father. Natasha has betrayed him."

Gaia stood in front of him. Her breath came so hard that her shoulders heaved. "No."

"Yes, I have the conclusive—"

Before George could finish his sentence, Gaia spun and headed for the door. George climbed to his feet and hurried after her.

"Gaia! Stay here! If you go back to that house, you'll only be giving them a chance to use you against your father!" There was no reply, and when George made it to the front door, there was no one in the street.

Gaia was gone.

She didn't like guns, but she had to admit that the weapon felt comforting. **her father's betrayer**

IT WAS STILL AWFULLY EARLY FOR A

Saturday, but the park was already coming alive. Kids were moving up and down the slides, their heavy coats making them look like little polar bears playing at the zoo. Vendors were setting up the hot dog carts. Steam rose from the

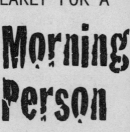

metal pans and frosted bottles of ketchup and sliced pickles. Across the sidewalk the chess players were already starting to assemble. Ed had to give them credit. As far as he was concerned, this was prime sleeping time.

However, Tatiana didn't seem to work on his schedule. She had been on the phone before seven, insisting that they go out and see the park Ed had talked about. Ed glanced over at her as he made his way along the sidewalk toward the arch at the center of the park. It didn't matter how pretty she was: if Tatiana turned out to be a morning person, he might have to kill her.

"I think maybe I like this place better than Central Park," said Tatiana. She stopped, flipped open her sketchbook, and made a few strokes on the paper. "It's not so large, but it's prettier."

"And Washington Square Park is eighty percent less likely to get you killed," Ed replied.

Tatiana looked at him with a puzzled expression for

a moment, then laughed. They walked on, passing under the arch and on toward the tables where the chess players passed the time. Two middle-aged men were in the middle of a game. Ed didn't have to watch them long to see that neither of them was really much of a player. Gaia could have taken either one out in five minutes.

A couple of the regulars, including the Pakistani cabdriver that Gaia used to play, were set up at tables by themselves. These practiced pros craned their necks, looking for anyone who might be willing to play a friendly game. Say for twenty dollars. Fifty, maybe, but only if you insisted.

"Who is that?" Tatiana asked.

Ed followed her pointing hand. Down at the end of the row of tables a very old man limped to his place. The gray-haired man carefully dusted the bench with a handkerchief before slowly sitting. Then he pulled out a red plastic figurine and perched it on the side of the table before setting down a worn chessboard and getting out the pieces.

"That's Zolov," said Ed. "He's a little off, but he plays good chess."

"Off?"

"Crazy." Ed did the finger-at-the-side-of-the-head twirl and wondered if it meant the same thing in Russian.

"Oh," said Tatiana. "But he has a very interesting face."

She sat down at a bench across the walk from the chess tables and began to sketch on her pad. Ed moved around to stand behind her. He watched in fascination as her slim, elegant fingers moved rapidly over the paper. There was a soft, constant scratch of the pencil. Tatiana's head was tilted a bit to the left, her mouth slightly open as she concentrated on her work, the tip of her pink tongue pressed against her teeth. She glanced up from time to time and watched as the old Ukrainian finished off his first opponent of the day.

As her pencil moved, Ed saw Zolov and the park around him gradually come to life on the page. Tatiana captured the trees in the background, the couples strolling in the distance, and even the tense concentration on Zolov's face as his wrinkled, rawboned hand reached out to advance a pawn. Every movement of Tatiana's pencil hand seemed to add more texture, more depth, more emotion to the simple black-and-white scene.

Finally she stopped, took one last look at the old chess player, then looked over her shoulder at Ed. "What do you think?" she asked.

Ed shook his head in wonder. "I think it's a classic," he said.

"Better than the skateboard?"

Ed rolled his eyes. "Very close."

Tatiana smiled at him. She grabbed the edge of the

paper and pulled it out of the pad. Then she stood and strolled down the sidewalk toward Zolov. Ed followed her, but not too closely. He saw Tatiana sit down at the bench and heard her say something in Russian.

The old man's eyes brightened. He replied to Tatiana with enthusiasm. His hands went out in sweeping gestures that took in the whole park, then in smaller moves about the battered chess set. Tatiana held out the sketch to Zolov. He took the paper and studied it for several seconds, his thick gray eyebrows drawn together. Then he suddenly leaned back in his seat and thrust the paper back to Tatiana.

For a moment Ed thought that the old man was upset, but as Tatiana walked away, he flashed a gap-toothed smile. "You come back soon," he called. "We play a game together!"

"I will," said Tatiana. She gave the man a little wave, then walked over to join Ed. "He liked my picture."

"Of course he did," said Ed. "After all, we're talking masterpiece. What did you say to him?"

Tatiana shrugged her thin shoulders. "That he was a good player. That he would do well playing the men in Gorky Park." She shrugged again. "I said some other things, but they weren't important."

Ed glanced at Zolov. The old man was still smiling. "They may not have been important to you, but they meant something to him. I think you're his new best friend. I've seen that guy in the park for years, and I've never seen him look this happy."

Tatiana bobbed her head, and a flush came over her cheeks. It took Ed a moment to realize she was blushing. "Come on," she said. "Don't we have more sights to see?"

Ed nodded, but he wasn't thinking about sights. He was thinking that Tatiana was perfect. She was funny and kind, and she liked Ed. He was thinking that even if he did still love Gaia Moore, nothing was ever going to come of that love. It was time to move on. It was time to take steps toward having that life A.G. he'd been thinking about. He reached up with one arm and pulled Tatiana up toward him. He pulled her face close to his with more force than he had intended until their lips were pressed together. Then he was kissing Tatiana, and it was all good.

GAIA STUMBLED THROUGH THE DOOR

of the apartment. She stood at the bottom of the stairs, swaying on her feet. It had been nearly thirty-six hours since she had slept. Pure emotion had kept her on her

Bat-Gaia

feet, but emotion was also draining. She felt hollow. Used up. Like a paper cup left along the roadway. But she didn't dare sleep. Not when she knew that they were watching her every minute. Not when she was right in the home of her father's betrayer.

Before she rested, she had to stop Loki.

If Natasha was a spy, that only made the job more important. More vital. Her father could be lured to his death at any moment. He might already be dead. No. She couldn't think that way.

Gaia turned toward the stairs and plodded upward. Find Loki. Find him soon. End it. Those thoughts had been running through her head for hours as the sky brightened between the big buildings and the nighttime turned into brilliant day. But hadn't she already been consumed by these thoughts for months?

She could pretend to have a normal life. That was a lie. She could pretend to be Bat-Gaia, beating up muggers and protecting the innocent. But that was a lie, too. She could slave over breaking some random code. Lie. She could be cruel to Ed or love him. It was all a lie.

The truth was that she had been running away. Gaia had hurried out to face a hundred fights, but she had been running away from the only fight that counted. She had been avoiding facing Loki and ending this once and for all.

She might be fearless, but at that moment she considered herself a coward.

Step one: Face Loki.

No, that wasn't right. To face him, she had to find him. Her uncle might reply to her e-mail and set up a meeting, but he might not. Even if he did, it might take days. Gaia couldn't wait. She needed to force things to happen. Now.

Okay, that was easy. If she couldn't find Loki, she could certainly find his spy. His assistant. The heartless bitch whom he had sent to catch her father. She could get *Natasha*. Then she would force Natasha to take her to Loki.

Gaia walked toward Natasha's room, blinking away sleep at each step. The bed was still neat. No one had slept here.

She probably spent the night with Loki. She must be sleeping with him. Convincing my father that she loves him, then sleeping with Loki. The thought should have made her furious, but she was too tired for fury. She needed a plan. She needed a way to capture Natasha and make her reveal everything she knew about Loki.

Gaia crossed the room and bent down to open the bottom drawer of the dresser. The gun was still there. She took it out, weighing the solid feel of it in her hand. She didn't like guns, but she had to admit that the weapon felt comforting. When Natasha saw the black hole of the barrel pointed her way, she would talk. But Gaia didn't intend to shoot Natasha. That she would save for Loki.

As she started to stand, Gaia caught a glimpse of the nightstand. The stand where the letters were hidden. All at once tears were streaming down her cheeks again. This time her throat didn't just get tight. Gaia exploded.

"Idiot!" she shouted at herself. "Did you think it could have a happy ending? Did you think someone could ever love you?" She tossed back her head and let the pain carry her past words, until her throat was raw with her sobbing and the tears dripped from the point of her chin.

It had only been a dream. A dream that was gone as quickly as it came. Gaia and her father and Natasha and Tatiana. All together like a family. It was only a dream. A stupid dream. Nothing worth crying over.

Only she couldn't stop.

Until she heard a sound coming from the stairway.

Gaia swallowed her last sob and stood statue still. In the sudden silence her ears rang and her heart beat in her throat.

A footstep on the stairs. Another.

She raised the gun. Two-hand stance. One foot pushed slightly back. Well balanced. Just as her father had taught her.

Another step.

Gaia aimed the gun at the level of the doorknob. Waist-level for Natasha. That was another of her father's instructions. Always keep a gun aimed at the center of the body. Don't go for anything fancy like a head shot; just make sure you connect with the target. If Natasha rushed her, Gaia could drop the gun and fight. If Natasha was carrying a weapon, Gaia could shoot. She was ready.

The footsteps reached the top of the stairs and started down the short hallway. Gaia waited.

A tall figure stepped into the doorway. At first Gaia was confused. She saw only a trench coat and legs. She raised her eyes. "Dad?" she said softly. The man took one step into the room, and Gaia instantly knew the truth. She raised the gun to point at his chest. "What a coincidence. I was just thinking about you."

The man stopped. He raised his hands slightly, like someone making a joke about being arrested. "I would appreciate it if you'd point that somewhere else," he said.

Gaia kept her aim. "I don't think so, Uncle Oliver. Oops, I mean, Loki."

Oliver shook his head. "I'm not a killer." He took another step.

With one quick movement of her thumb Gaia brought back the hammer on the revolver. The chambers of the pistol turned, lining up a bullet to the barrel with a satisfying, solid click. "Stop. There."

Oliver stopped.

"What are you doing here?" asked Gaia. "Looking for your partner? Your girlfriend?"

"I was looking for you." Oliver slowly lowered his hands. "I have something very important I need to tell you."

Gaia laid her finger against the trigger. It didn't matter what he said. She knew Oliver was Loki. He had to be. This was the chance she had been waiting for. One pull of the trigger, and Loki was gone. "I don't want to hear anything you have to say."

"It's about your father."

The revolver was instantly twice as heavy in her hands, and the air in the room turned thick. Gaia let her hand drop a few inches as she struggled to get in enough air to talk. "Has something happened to my father?"

"Not exactly." Oliver looked at her with an expression that Gaia couldn't begin to read. "Gaia, I know this is going to be hard for you, but things weren't always perfect between Katia and my brother. I think they were truly in love at first, and at the end. But that love wasn't constant through all the years of their marriage."

"What are you talking about?" asked Gaia. "Is my father all right?"

Oliver nodded. "So far as I'm aware, my brother is fine. I believe he's right here in the city."

Gaia brought the gun back up. "Are you holding him hostage?"

"Nothing of the sort." The idea seemed to shock Oliver. "Gaia, you have some extraordinary ideas about me."

This was the time. If her father was safe, Gaia could take out Loki now and make sure he stayed safe. There might be more agents out there, but without Loki they wouldn't be a threat. Cut off the head, kill the snake. She aimed carefully.

"Gaia," Oliver said slowly. "There was a period about eighteen years ago in which Tom and Katia were separated."

Her finger tightened on the trigger.

"During that time I went to Katia. At first I was only trying to comfort her, but later. . ." He shrugged. "Later it became something more."

The hammer of the revolver began to pull back above the firing pin.

"When Tom and Katia got back together, we were both very careful never to mention our time together. But Gaia, there's something you have to know."

Squeeze evenly. Don't jerk. Keep your aim.

"Gaia," said Oliver. "I'm your father."

The small sight at the front of the gun was

centered on his chest. Her finger was tight against the trigger. One more pound of pressure. One more ounce, and Loki would be dead.

Gaia closed her eyes and pulled the trigger.

There was no shot. Just a hard, dry, worthless click as the hammer came down hard on the firing pin above an empty cylinder. I stood there with my eyes closed for a long time. I can't say how long. It seemed like hours. Like eternity. It was probably more like thirty seconds. When I opened my eyes, he was gone. My chance to kill Loki, my chance to salvage my piss-poor excuse for a life, was over.

It's a lie. This Darth Vader thing he's trying to pull. It absolutely, positively cannot be true. Not in this universe or any other universe. I know he's the killer. I know he's Loki. I know he killed my mother and my friends and ruined my life. There's no way he can be my father.

No way in hell.

here is a
sneak peek of
Fearless™ #22:
ALONE

GAIA STEPPED OUT OF THE HOT AND

De Facto sticky subway station and into an equally hot and sticky morning. She was in no mood for this pea soup weather, especially so early in the season. Lexington Avenue was already cluttered with strollers, nannies, and purebred dogs, and of course, its signature residents, the perfect people, spending wads of money on Lexus strollers and canine cologne.

Downtown, where Gaia used to live, the buildings were smaller and the people a little more on the ball. Within blocks of her brownstone were immigrant neighborhoods with streets just brimming with personality. Exotic smells drifted out of shops whose signs were handwritten in different languages. Chinatown. Little Italy. Up here, everything looked as bland and generic as a J. Crew catalog. Gaia like to refer to it as Little Connecticut.

She had a job to do this morning, and she wasn't looking forward to it. Staying with Natasha and her daughter, Tatiana, was fine as a stopgap measure. It was a place to crash, and at this point that was all Gaia wanted. But her conversation with George Niven kept echoing in her skull, and she had to do something about it. According to George, Natasha was nothing but a snake whose sole purpose was nabbing Gaia's father.

Now she had to get her butt up to the apartment, confront Natasha, and get her the hell away from her dad.

Of course, there was that nagging question of why she owed Tom anything. It was a question that held permanent residence in the back of her mind but also kept a rental in the forefront for just such an occasion.

Then again, Gaia had to admit, the letters Tom had given her—sheaves and sheaves of paper dating back to when she was twelve, detailing how much he loved her, missed her, and hated to have to leave her, neatly typed and hand-signed every single day that they hadn't been together—were pretty convincing evidence that he, at least, gave a crap where she woke up and who she hung out with, even if he had disappeared for most of her adolescence. So Gaia had to figure that even if he wasn't her biological father, as her uncle had recently claimed, he at least had a stake in her well-being, despite the fact that it was Oliver who appeared, `like magic,` whenever she most needed him.

She stepped into the ornate foyer of the building. Her sneakers made a squeaking noise on the marble floor as she headed toward the elevator button. She studied her reflection in the thin strip of brass behind the button. High forehead, dirty blond hair hanging to her waist, and an angry set to her jaw. This was the face that Tom thought about every day? Gaia wasn't convinced. But if getting to the bottom of the situation meant, de facto, uncovering Natasha's sinister plot, then so be it.

Downtime

IT WAS AMAZING, TOM MOORE mused, that you could be surrounded by so much physical beauty and still be dealing with ugly, menacing danger. He stepped out on the terrace of his hotel room, scanning the white beach and turquoise water for any sign of spies or hit men, but saw only frolicking tourists and hotel employees, dressed in spanking-white tunics, carrying piles of white fluffy towels. For a moment he allowed himself to relax as Natasha came up behind him and wound her arms around his torso, caressing his chest as she kissed the very center of his back. She had just flown in from New York the night before.

"I guess I didn't have to reserve my own room after all," she said.

"Not necessarily," he said as he turned toward her and put his arms around her neck. "I could think of a few different ways to put it to use." Their first night together had been filled with more passion than he'd felt since Katia's death, followed by the first full night's sleep he'd had since then, too.

"Perhaps a little later—now we have work to do." She sighed, pouring coffee from the tall silver decanter that room service had placed outside their door.

Tom just gazed out the window.

"You are thinking about Gaia?" Natasha asked.

"She's so far away," Tom said, stepping inside, leaving the sliding doors wide open so that the humid tropical air filled the room. He picked up the delicate coffee cup in one hand and slugged down the rich black liquid. "I don't like being where I can't rush in if something happens to her."

"But you're almost never near enough to her—physically, I mean—to do that," Natasha pointed out as she stirred two lumps of sugar into her coffee and broke a biscotti in half. "It must be torment. I don't even like being away from Tatiana for a weekend."

"It's been like having an arm cut off," Tom agreed. "If I can only take care of Loki, I won't have to worry that just by being near her, I'm putting her life in danger."

"Then that's what we are going to do," Natasha said, with such conviction Tom believed they'd really do it this time.

"At least I know we're close," he said. "Somehow that takes the edge off the stress. I don't remember when I've ever felt so . . ."

"Carefree?"

"Not exactly. But something approaching it." He put down his coffee and stroked his finger softly along the delicate flesh that peeked from the top of Natasha's bathrobe.

Tom's Blackberry beeped. He jumped, suddenly realizing how distracted he was from his job, and broke away to see what the minicomputer had to say to him. "What is it?" Natasha asked, seeing a shadow cross his face.

"There's a delay," he answered her. "The operative we're supposed to track isn't going to be here for another day."

Tom felt the familiar clutch in his gut, telling him he could do nothing but lay low till someone, somewhere, did their job. He hated downtime; action quieted the noise in his head. Yet around the edges he felt his anxiety soften a bit. What the hell. If he had to waste a day, he was glad to have Natasha's company.

HEATHER BOUNCED INTO THE STARBUCKS

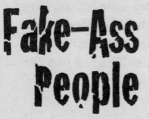

on her way to school. It was time to meet Josh, and every nerve-ending in her body was alert with anticipation.

He had already ordered up a

grande for her, remembering the dash of cinnamon and extra foam. She loved how attentive he was. Suddenly being slighted by Sam and Ed in favor of Gaia didn't matter—Josh was more intriguing than either one of them had been, and he was interested only in her.

"Good morning," she said.

"Same to you, gorgeous," he answered, nuzzling into her hair so that she shivered with the delicious warmth of it. "And what's on the schedule for this hot student body?"

"I predict a pop quiz on *Catcher in the Rye* in English class today," she said. "Just to make sure we're all keeping up with the adventures of Holden Caulfield."

"Good old Holden," Josh said.

"Yeah, I read it in seventh grade." Heather shook her head. "It's brilliant. I love it when he talks about everyone being—"

"—a goddamn phony?" Josh finished the sentence with her. They both laughed.

All Holden's talk of the fake-ass people he met at prep school really hit home for Heather. Her own "friends" were like cardboard cutouts, yapping about their paraffin manicures and Brazilian bikini waxes and the next party in the Hamptons. Yet even knowing how lame it all was, she still had to play the game. Hell, she was the captain.

"The thing I love about us is that we're always on the same page."

Us. Heather did an instant audio replay. She loved the sound of that word so much, she could have recorded it onto a loop and listened to it all day.

"I guess we are." She was twinkling.

"Well, if that's the case, then you must be feeling as anxious as I am to get you started on those fearless injections."

Suddenly the twinkling faded. She looked at Josh, gazing deeply into his eyes. It was clear that he really cared about her. That he had her best interests in mind. But she still felt unsure about the whole fearless issue.

"But what if something goes wrong?" she asked.

"Have you been taking the pills?"

"Of course," Heather said, opening her bag so Josh could see the prescription bottle.

Josh made a sympathetic face. "If you're taking the pills, then nothing should go wrong. Trust me."

Josh put his arms around her and dragged both Heather and her chair closer into the circle of his arms and legs. She giggled and nestled into his muscular warmth, letting her mind wander into a reverie: She and Gaia facing off, Gaia focused and determined until Heather began fighting back with amazing speed. Then she saw Gaia's face fall apart like a puzzle, confused and startled by Heather's new grace, speed, and bravery. Heather finished her off with a kick to the gut, and Gaia fell. In her daydream Heather turned to see Josh, who nodded, took her by the hand, and drew her in for a passionate smooch.

Maybe Josh was right. Maybe trust was the answer.

ED LAY ON HIS BACK ON A TABLE,

his legs pumping at a beeping machine. He was trying to concentrate on making his legs work on the weird StairMaster thing, but mostly he was trying to keep his mind on training and out of the gutter.

Stupid Crutches

"So, uh . . . where's Brian again?"

"He's on vacation," said Lydia, his new physical therapist. "You're stuck with me."

Stuck? Lydia was hot. Which in any other setting would be a fine way for Ed to take his mind off his confusion over Gaia and Tatiana. But in this case it was cause for distraction. Ed tried to think about baseball.

"Feel the burn?" Lydia asked.

"Sheee-yeah," Ed grumbled.

"All right. We have to talk." Lydia took her hand off Ed's upper leg.

Thank God, he thought.

Lydia glared at Ed, and he wondered if his over-active hormones were showing in some way he didn't know about. *Hey, I'm just a healthy red-blooded American*, he thought.

"Do you want to tell me why you're still on those crutches when you clearly don't need them anymore?"

What?

"Uh, hello, Earth to medical professional," Ed said, rolling his eyes. "I was in a massive skateboarding accident? Big hill, no brakes, Ed meets gravel? Two years in a wheelchair? Is any of this ringing a bell?"

Lydia laughed and turned to face him. "Yeah. But that's all in the past now. You've progressed a lot farther than you're willing to admit, but you won't take that first step."

Ed stared at her, flabbergasted.

"I see this a lot," Lydia said. "The body wants to get up and walk out of the chair, but the mind is still scared. Ed, there's nothing to be scared of. You can walk without your crutches, and if you let yourself, you can move on from your accident and all the pain it brought you."

Ed blinked. "Is that true? Why didn't Brian tell me?"

"He was probably just being soft on you," Lydia said. "Hoping you'd figure it out on your own. But I'm

11

not like him. I want you to take a break from the crutches—before I see you next."

A break? Ed wanted to toss the stupid crutches into a vat of sulfuric acid. But did Lydia really know what she was talking about? Ed concentrated, quieting his mind so that he could really feel his legs. There was that same cold, numb feeling, like when his feet were asleep and he couldn't quite walk till they woke up. But maybe it was all in his head.

Maybe he *was* ready to walk alone?